D0912736

Praise for R. F. McClure's

Winder Hollow

McClure writes a timeless love story as old as the Appalachian Mountains and as fresh as today's reader's demand.

---Barb Henney
2009 Pulse Magazine
Flash Fiction Award Winner

Order this book online at www.trafford.com
or email orders@trafford.com

Most Trafford titles are also available at major online book retailers.

© Copyright 2010 R. F. McClure.
All rights reserved. No part of this publication may be reproduced, stored in a retrieval system, or
transmitted, in any form or by any means, electronic, mechanical, photocopying, recording, or
otherwise, without the written prior permission of the author.

Printed in Victoria, BC, Canada.

ISBN: 978-1-4269-2706-5 (sc)
ISBN: 978-1-4269-2762-1 (eb)

*Our mission is to efficiently provide the world's finest, most comprehensive book publishing
service, enabling every author to experience success. To find out how to publish your book, your
way, and have it available worldwide, visit us online at www.trafford.com*

Trafford rev. 2/26/10

 www.trafford.com

North America & international
toll-free: 1 888 232 4444 (USA & Canada)
phone: 250 383 6864 ♦ fax: 812 355 4082

R. F. McClure

***

Winder Hollow

" To Karen "
Enjoy the story
and the adventure.

R. F. McClure

This book is dedicated to my wife, Mary Ann, my daughters, Anne and Mary, who believed in my dream of a better way of life.

And:

My talented editor and friend, Marsha Butler, with her keen eye and sense of humor nudged me in the right direction.

Author's Note

Winder Hollow, a work of fiction, is deep-seated in folklore and family drama within the West Virginia Mountains.

I was fortunate to have a family that was willing to share a life of self-sacrifice and hardships to prove we could survive the rigors of mountain life. We embraced our new lifestyle to the fullest, knowing that everyday on the mountain would offer a new life experience. Throughout the years, the generosity of our neighbors would sustain us in many ways. Their simple, time honored ways of surviving in the mountains, served us well in the twelve years we lived the old-ways, enjoying mountain fare with them and listening intently as they wove the magic of their tales around us. The years spent there inspired my writing. A writer couldn't ask for better memories with which to write endless stories about the mountain people. Their lives are colorful, the mountains are inspiring, and the natural beauty and solitude are Heaven on earth.

In *Winder Hollow,* I have endeavored to keep alive the memories of the courageous, early mountain settlers who are a part of our American heritage.

Chapter 1

Appalachian Mountains, 1964

The storm clouds hung heavy over the mountains of West Virginia. It didn't look as if there would be any end to the weather that had plagued the area for over three weeks. The creeks had overflowed their banks, mountain roads had washed out, and life was dismal at best.

The mountain folks up the hollows had the toughest time of all. The torrential rains had caused some of the steep mountain slopes to shift, and danger was all around them. Most had to keep to their small cabins and hope for the best, but one poor soul was fighting a losing battle, if she didn't get help soon.

Alma Lee Holcomb, a young woman of nineteen, lay in her sweat-soaked bed, writhing in pain. She knew something was terribly wrong but had no idea what. She had been in bed for two days, unable to eat, let alone keep anything in her stomach. The old bucket beside her handmade bed reeked of stale vomit. The heat from the wood-burning stove didn't help her fever torn body. But the cold rain had made everything unbearably damp, and without the heat she would be wracked with uncontrollable shakes.

Jacob, her younger brother, had been gone for well over an hour in search of Granny Harris—the local Healer. She knew it would take some time for him to fetch Granny, but what could be taking so long? She lay on her cornhusk mattress, her stringy, red hair plastered to the tattered quilt. The constant rocking of her legs back-and-forth was the only thing she could think of to keep her mind off the excruciating pain. She moaned non-stop. "Jacob, Jacob," she pleaded, "where is ya? I is powerful sick an' I shore do needs Granny."

Chapter 2

Early morning darkness blanketed the hollow. The cold, wind-driven rain pounded Jacob at every step, as he stumbled through the slick mountain mud toward yet another neighbor's cabin.

He had scoured the hollow in search of Granny Harris for over an hour. He couldn't find her. Frantically he searched. *Where could she be?*

Jacob had grown up in Winder Hollow, but even at the age of fifteen, he had never had the opportunity to explore all of it. His years of attending the one-room schoolhouse and working hard along side his paw hadn't left much idle time for exploring.

The hollow was large, a mile wide in spots and three-and-a-half miles long. Where the mountain slopes met the wide open valley, the mountain ridge rose nearly eight-hundred feet above the valley floor. It meandered in a northerly direction and at times opened up into smaller side hollows. Ultimately, the ridgeline made a sweeping curve where it formed the head of the hollow. The ridgeline made a "U" turn and headed back south, where it dropped down to the valley floor, creating the opening to the hollow.

Over a hundred families lived in the hollow. Most had built their cabins on the relatively flat to rolling land of the hollow floor, others on the steep, heavily-forested mountain slopes. Some lived in solitude within the smaller side hollows.

Thirty yards from the cabin, the heavy haze that blanketed the hollow shifted from a gust of wind, and Jacob spotted the welcoming glow of a kerosene lamp from within.

He stomped the thick mud from his boots and stepped onto the cabin porch. He heard the shuffling of feet, in response to his rapid pounding.

The door opened wide. Mrs. Sparks held the lantern high to see who had come to her home at such an hour.

As the yellow glow of the lantern pierced the darkness, her quizzical look changed to a wide grin.

"Well, if it ain't Jacob Holcomb! What ya doin' out in this kinda weather? Look at ya. Ya are shakin' like a leaf and soakin' wet. Git yurself inside an' warm up some."

"Yes, Ma'am, but I can't be stayin' long, 'cause I has ta find Granny Harris."

"What ya needin' Granny fer, this time a mornin'?"

"My sister, Alma Lee, is right sick. She hain't been able ta eat fer a couple of days an' she's throwin' up somethin' fierce. Has ya heard anythin' 'bout where Granny could be? I checked her place right off, but she twern't there."

"Ya can stop yer search, 'cause she passed by here not more than an hour ago. I spotted her an' that old mule of hers headin' up the holler. I had jest stepped out onta the porch ta pack in some firewood fer my cook stove. I hollered out ta her, an' she pulled her mule up short. I had ta holler right hard ta be heard over the downpour.

I asked her, 'Granny, what in tarnation is ya doin' out in this here storm?' She prodded her mule ta git a might closer, tilted her head back, looked out from under that old floppy hat a hers ta see who had done the hollerin'. She shore did look all done in, but managed ta tell me where she was a headin'. She said that Williams woman were about ta give birth ta her fifth child, an' her man had got word fer her ta come quick."

Jacob broke his silence. "Mrs. Sparks, I haint never been past the fishin' pond that's up the holler apiece. Can ya give me directions ta the Williams' place?"

"I surely can. Take a seat over here at the table. I'll pour ya a cup a hot coffee. It'll take the chill offa ya."

Holding the hot mug of coffee with cupped hands, Jacob welcomed the warmth as he sipped the delicious black brew. He listened carefully to the woman's directions.

"Onct ya git ta the pond, work yer way 'round ta the right side. Ya will see the trail ta the Williams' place. They's 'bout half-a-mile further up ta the head of the holler. Their cabin is agin the side of the mountain. Ya can't hardly miss it."

Jacob took the last swallow of coffee and pushed away from the table. "I surely do thank ya fer the coffee an' directions, Mrs. Sparks."

Just as he was about to open the cabin door, she stopped him. "Hold on there, Jacob. I got me some fresh cornbread bakin' in the oven. Ya look like ya could use a big piece 'bout now."

With hot pad in hand, she pulled open the oven door. The sweet aroma that filled the room made Jacob's mouth water.

She sliced and removed two generous pieces of the steaming cornbread. She quickly wrapped both in a spare cloth and handed them to him.

With a knowing grin, she said, "I kinda figured a growin' boy could use an extra slice fer yer trip back, onct ya find Granny."

She opened the door for Jacob, giving him a reassuring pat on his shoulder. "I sure hope Alma Lee gits ta feelin' better, Jacob. Don't ya be worrin' none, 'cause Granny will set her right in no time."

Jacob thanked her again and stepped off the porch into the unrelenting downpour.

He devoured the first piece of cornbread within minutes of leaving the cabin. The remaining piece he tucked safely in his jacket pocket. He pulled his hat down tight on his head, turned his collar up and leaned into the wind as the bitter, cold rain stung his cheeks.

True to the directions he was given, he found the path to the Williams' cabin. He followed it at a grueling pace. Fifteen minutes later, just as the morning sun made an effort to penetrate the thick cloud cover, he reached the head of the hollow, drenched to the bone and exhausted.

He leaned against a nearby tree to catch his breath and sucked in the cool, fresh morning air, as he searched the mountain side for any sign of a cabin.

He caught a whiff of smoke that blew down from the mountain slope. Shielding his eyes from the pelting rain, he surveyed the thick canopy of trees. A sudden lull in the storm allowed him to spot a curl of smoke rising from the cabin's chimney.

Jacob reluctantly pushed himself away from the tree and headed directly toward the telltale smoke.

Within minutes, he located the well-worn path winding its way up the rugged mountain slope. He braced himself for the demanding climb up the steep, muddy trail that would take him to the Williams' cabin and, hopefully, Granny Harris.

Chapter 3

After what seemed like an eternity to Alma Lee, the door to the cabin burst open. Jacob, chilled to the bone, and gasping for breath, entered the stifling, hot cabin. The heat and stench that permeated the place made him nauseous. He propped open the cabin door for some much needed fresh air, before he became sick himself.

He crossed the room to the bed where Alma Lee lay moaning. He placed a cool damp rag on her forehead. Feeling the soothing relief, she opened her eyes, and in a hoarse voice, asked, "Did ya find Granny?"

Jacob knelt next to the bed, gently lifted his sister up and offered her a sip of fresh spring water. She took a small sip, swished the remainder around in her mouth to rid herself of the foul taste that had accumulated there and spit it into the nearby bucket.

Jacob turned the soaked, sweat-stained pillow over and lowered her head onto it. He held her hand and stroked her forehead softly. "Don't ya worry none, Alma Lee, 'cause Granny will be comin' real soon. She were way up in the head of the holler helpin' that Williams woman give birth. That woman was a screamin' a whole heap more than ya was. Granny says the poor child is comin' out back'ards, an' that ain't good. Granny be prayin' her poor old mule can make the trip down here with the way the old mountain mud is stickin' ta everythin' an' makin' travel durn right nervous."

Jacob turned his head to the window as the raging wind blew down the hollow with a gust that shook the cabin. He watched as the trees near the cabin shuddered from the onslaught. Somewhere close a tree crashed to the forest floor. He turned to assure his sister that everything would be alright. Alma Lee was sound asleep.

Jacob tucked the quilt in around his sister and climbed the wooden ladder to his small loft bedroom. He changed into clean, dry clothes.

He carried his wet, mud-smeared clothes from the loft, hung them on the nearby clothesline and settled in close to the comforting warmth of the wood-burning stove.

He looked over at his sister and watched the rise and fall of the old quilt, as she labored for every breath.

It was times like this when he missed his maw and paw the most. The accident that took their lives, a few years earlier, had made instant orphans of them. But he and his sister had survived with the help of their neighbors and lots of hard work.

Jacob surveyed the cabin with a keen eye. A feeling of melancholy spread over him. Paw had laid the rough, hand-hewn logs some twenty years earlier. He admired the dovetail cuts that held each log in place. His father's work was second to none.

To the right of where Alma lay sleeping, the massive, stone fireplace dominated the wall of the living area. His paw had laid up the flat mountain stones, painstakingly placing each stone in just the right spot. Jacob had always loved the many shapes and hues of the stone his father picked to build the fireplace.

Paw had told him several times that a fireplace was not complete until it had been crowned with a useful and decorative mantle. And what a beautiful mantle he had built! The large hand-hewed slab of Tulip poplar was six inches thick and a foot wide. It ran the entire width of the eight-foot fireplace. The dogwood blossoms Paw carved into the front of the mantle were a testament to his father's keen eye for perfection. Many years of natural aging combined with the heat and smoke from the fireplace had given the wood a deep, chestnut-brown patina that accentuated the intricate details of the carvings.

With his eyelids drooping, Jacob's thoughts slipped back to the days when he sat at the kitchen table and watched his mother prepare their meals. The aroma of the wholesome foods she cooked filled the cabin, tantalizing his senses and causing his stomach to growl.

He sniffed the air now and was rewarded with a lingering aroma that had permeated deep into the fiber of the cabin's logs—a reminder of long-ago meals.

His eyes shifted to the loft. It brought back memories of his early years, growing up with his sister.

Anticipating the birth of their first baby, Alma Lee, Jacob's paw set about adding a small bedroom onto the cabin for him and his wife. Alma Lee would sleep with them in the bedroom until she was three. Then she would move to her own bed in the loft.

Four years later, Jacob was born. He too spent his first three years sleeping in Maw and Paw's bedroom.

Jacob would end up sharing the loft with his sister for several years. This arrangement worked well for the both of them, especially on cold winter nights. He would sneak from his corner of the loft and climb in bed with Alma Lee. They would snuggle up and share the much-needed, extra body heat.

When Alma Lee was near her thirteenth birthday, Maw announced that since Alma Lee had become a young woman, it was only right for her to have a place of her own. That very day, Alma Lee's bed was lowered from the loft and placed in the corner to the left of the fireplace, where it remained to this day.

Jacob's eyelids were getting heavier by the moment. He looked over at his sister one more time, leaned his chair back against the wall and fell fast asleep. The warmth of the stove had won the battle with fatigue.

Three long hours later, Jacob was awakened by the faint sound of a mule's hooves as they clicked on the rocky, rain-soaked path. The rain and wind had not let up one bit during his much-needed rest. He tipped his chair noisily to the floor and rushed outside to help Granny down from her perch atop the mule. Jacob could see that Granny and the mule were all done in. Grabbing the mule's halter, he watched as Granny headed up the steep path to the cabin.

She hunched her shoulders, leaned into the cold, wind-driven torrent and struggled to maintain her footing in the ankle-deep mud.

Her head bent low, she plodded ahead as the rain pelted her tattered felt hat and ran down the back of her old slicker.

When she reached the cabin porch, she steadied herself against the railing and stomped the caked mud from her boots.

At the cabin door, she turned, pushed her rain- drenched spectacles back in place, and in a breathless voice, said, "Boy, ya see ta my mule; she's had a mighty tough day."

When she turned, Jacob saw exhaustion etched heavily on her weather-worn face. He shouted out to her over the howl of the wind. "Don't ya be frettin' none, Granny, 'cause I got some good oats in the barn, an' I'll rub'er down fer ya."

Granny Harris had been healing folks in Winder Hollow for most of her adult life. Her mamaw had taught her maw all about healing with the local herbs and remedies passed down from generation to generation in the mountains of West Virginia. Granny was next in line to become the Healer of the hollow. She was eager to learn all her maw had to teach. With her maw's untimely passing, just short of Granny's eighteenth birthday, she became the Healer of the hollow. She accepted her position as the mountain Healer with pride and vowed to do right by the folks in Winder Hollow—the place of her birth, seventy-eight years ago.

Granny smelled the sickness, even before she opened the cabin door. It was her calling to do what was needed. She braced herself and entered the small cabin.

The heat inside the cabin fogged up her spectacles and made her feel faint. During the two-mile ride down the hollow, the cold, damp rain had chilled her to the bone. The cabin's intense heat was a shock to her aging body.

She removed her old, worn slicker, slipped off her boots, wiped her spectacles on her shirttail and approached the bed, where Alma Lee lay moaning. In a soft, soothing voice, she said, "Child, old Granny be here ta help ya with y'ur sickness."

Alma Lee tried to sit up and offer a slight smile, as Granny came into focus.

"Ya best be still child an' let me have a closer look at ya."

"I kinda thought maybe it be time fer my curse ta come 'round, but it twern't so," Alma Lee offered in a strained voice. "I knowed it had ta be somethin' right bad, an' that's why I had Jacob come fetch ya."

Granny, as gently as she could, removed Alma Lee's soiled dress. She probed Alma Lee's stomach in the spots where it seemed to hurt the most. With the tips of her fingers, she pressed down hard on the right side of Alma Lee's stomach then released the pressure with a quick jerk of her hands. Alma Lee screamed and almost flopped herself from the small, narrow bed. She passed out cold.

Jacob heard the scream above the howl of the storm. He raced to the cabin and threw open the door. Alma Lee lay motionless on her bed. "Is she gonna die?"

Granny held up her hand, motioning him to stay back. "Ya best just sit y'urself down over there by the stove an' dry out some. Y'ur sister ain't 'bout ta be passin' on anytime soon. She is powerful sick, an' we has got ta git her down ta the settlement right quick."

Jacob ran his hands through his thick, unruly shock of hair, as he paced the floor.

Granny could see he had worked himself up into a frenzy. "Jacob, ya best grab hold of y'urself."

With that he stopped pacing and turned to look Granny in the eye. "Is ya sure we's got ta take her? Alma Lee hain't never set foot outta the holler from the day she were born."

"Boy, there is somethin' we all don't have any choice 'bout, an' this here is one of 'em things. We has got ta git y'ur sister outta here right now, an' this is what I need ya ta do. Ya go git that Quentin boy from 'cross the crick, an' have him run down the holler an' fetch old Hillard. Ya have him tell Hillard ta hitch up his wagon an' git up ta the Holcomb cabin right quick. We's got a sick child up here an' we has ta git her down ta the settlement. Now, ya best git goin'"

Jacob grabbed his wet coat and pulled his hat on. Before he made it to the door, Granny stopped him. "Take my poor, old mule with ya, an' onct ya git Quentin on his way, ya head on up the holler an' find Tolliver Hicks. Ya tell him Granny Harris needs a small jar of his best shine. We's got ta dull Alma Lee's pain some."

Jacob turned to her, a puzzled look on his face. "Granny, I hain't ever been ta Tolliver's place but onct in my life, an' it were more than three years ago when Paw done took me. I don't rightly know if I can find the place."

She let out a small "Harrumph."

"Don't ya be worried 'bout findin' old Tolliver. He'll hear ya comin' long afore ya see hide-nor-hair of him. His still is way up the second side holler from here. Ya jest foller the path that meanders 'long side of the crick, but take care, 'cause it gits right narrow an' dangerous. Don't ya be wastin' no time, ya hear? Alma Lee needs some relief from her misery."

Chapter 4

With the reins held tight in his trembling hands, Jacob guided the mule carefully up the steep, rugged trail. Several times the mule lost her footing and threatened to send them crashing into the raging creek below. He shuddered at the thought of it. He tightened his grip on the reins, leaned forward and spoke softly to her, while he gently patted her neck. "Ya jest take yer time, old mule. We has got ta git that shine, but I know ya don't want ta fall down in that there crick anymore than I do."

Several anxious moments later, the trail made a sharp bend around a large outcropping of rock. He spotted a large man through the misty haze as the man stepped from behind the rocks and in a deep mountain voice, said, "Who are ya, an' what ya want'n?" Jacob then heard the *click,* as the gun was pointed right at him.

The mule dug all four hooves deep into the sodden earth and laid her ears back in fright as the man hollered out. Jacob felt the hairs on the back of his neck bristle, and in a quavering voice, said, "I-I'm J-J-Jacob H-Holcomb, an' I'm lookin' fer Tolliver Hicks."

"Well! Ya done found him. What ya want'n?"

Still reeling from the man's sudden appearance, Jacob managed a weak reply. "Granny Harris sent me. . ."

Tollivar cut him off abruptly. "I knowed that, y'ur settin' her mule. What Granny be needin'?"

Jacob knew time was a wasting. He gathered his courage and plowed forward. "My sister, Alma Lee, is powerful sick, an' Granny says we needs a small jar a y'ur best shine. We has ta take her down ta the settlement, but she needs somethin' ta dull the pain afore she can travel."

Jacob heard the man uncock his gun. Tollivar motioned to Jacob. "Ya jest tether the mule ta the tree there, an' foller me."

Jacob did as he was told and headed out after the large man. He couldn't believe how easily Tolliver moved through the thick brush without making a sound. Jacob had to trot just to keep up with him.

After a rough five-minute walk, they burst into a small clearing. Jacob took in the surroundings at a glance, and spotted a large, dented, copper still. Scattered about were many gallon jugs. Some were filled with fresh shine from Tolliver's still. Not far from the still, stood two fifty-five gallon drums full of a foul smelling mixture of sour mash. An old rubber hose snaked its way from the still up through the rocks to a pool of water just below a small waterfall. He knew it had something to do with the making of moonshine, but wasn't about to ask.

Without a word, Tollivar disappeared into a small lean-to near the waterfall. He brought back a pint mason jar from his own personal stash and handed the moonshine to Jacob. It was the first time he had gotten a good look at the man. Not only was he a large raw-boned man, but his deep-set, dark eyes that peered out from under his tattered old hat, looked right through him. Jacob felt a chill run down his spine. Tolliver's long, grizzled beard was heavily stained with smears of old tobacco juice. Jacob knew, at a glance, this man was not to be taken lightly.

Tolliver abruptly turned him around and pointed the way back down the trail. "Ya jest keep y'ur eyes up offa the ground a bit an' ya can foller the old slash marks on them trees. The old mule be waitin' fer ya." In a softer tone Tolliver added, "I'm right sorry 'bout y'ur maw and paw."

Jacob walked about five yards down the trail thinking about what the man had said. He turned to thank him for the shine and what he had said about Maw and Paw. Tollivar was nowhere in sight. He had vanished into the thick haze without a sound.

Chapter 5

Jacob stopped several times to rest Granny's mule, before he finally made it back to the cabin. Waiting there was Hillard's team of mules and wagon ready to take his sister to the settlement.

Inside the cabin, Jacob noticed Granny had cleaned up Alma Lee and had changed her clothes. Two feed sacks lay on the wooden table.

Hillard sat close to the wood stove, trying to dry off. He nodded as Jacob looked his way, spit a stream of tobacco juice into the nearby ash scuttle, wiped his lips with his shirt sleeve and mumbled, "Hey Jacob," and continued whittling on the piece of firewood he held in his large hands.

Granny gave a sigh of relief when she spotted him and took the jar of moonshine he offered. She poured some into an old cup and coaxed Alma Lee to sit up and take a small sip of the clear liquid. As the moonshine trickled down her throat, Alma Lee grimaced, let out a hoarse cough and said, "Granny, I hain't never touched hard licker afore, an' it done burnt somethin' fierce."

Granny gently patted her hand, brushed her forehead lightly and said, "Child, ya jest take a little sip now an' then, an' ya'll feel much better. I knowed it is hard fer ya ta understand, but we has got ta git ya outta here, an' this here shine will help ya make the trip."

While Granny tended his sister, Jacob pulled out a chair from the kitchen table and sat down. He turned to speak to Hillard, but instead, just sat there in silence watching him chip away at the stick of firewood.

Jacob never tired of admiring the size of the man who sat quietly whittling. Hillard was a tall man who had to duck to enter their cabin. His broad shoulders sat on a massive body of solid muscle. The man was known throughout the hollow for his brute strength. Hillard's large calloused hands were a testament to his years of hard work as a woodsman. The man's size could intimidate most folks he met. But his round, boyish face with its ever present smile and the twinkle in his large, brown eyes told the true story of this gentle giant.

Shifting his eyes back to the table, Jacob peered into both of the feed sacks that lay before him. In one sack were some of his clothes. With a curious look, he turned to Granny. "What's my clothes doin' in one of these here pokes?"

With her hand pressed to the small of her back and the other pushing against her knee, Granny managed to stand upright. She let out a low groan. She turned to face him, wiped the beads of sweat from her brow, then shuffled over to the table and sat down across from him. She tucked a few loose strands of damp gray hair into place, and then began to speak in a slow, tired voice. "I has decided that ya will have ta help Hillard git y'ur sister ta the settlement. He is goin' ta be needin' some help, plus I can't be leavin' these folks here in the holler without a healer. Besides, that poor Williams woman hain't doin' so good after the birthin' of her baby."

Jacob's head shot up with a quick jerk, as he looked her right in the eyes. The look on his face was one of pure fright, and he blurted out, "Granny, ya knowed I hain't never been ta the settlement afore. I don't know if I could hardly stand bein' around all them folks down there."

She reached over and put a firm hand on his shoulder. "Boy," she said, "this is somethin' ya has got ta do, an' that is all there is ta it. Old Hillard, here, has been on many trips such as this one, an' he knows where y'ur goin'. Besides, ya must be almost sixteen by now, an' it's 'bout time ya got outa this old holler.

My second cousin, Mamie, lives on this side of the settlement an' she will see y'ur sister gits ta the hospital. I believe she has got ta have an operation ta remove her appendix. Ya an' Hillard will be stayin' at her place 'till Alma Lee gits better."

Once Granny stopped talking, Hillard looked over at the two of them. He could see the stress etched on Granny's face, as she propped her tired head up with both hands and closed her eyes. Hillard closed his jackknife, slipped it into his coverall pocket, and tossed the piece of wood onto the woodpile. He stood up to his full six-feet seven inches and brushed the wood chips from the front of his overalls. In his usual slow drawl, he said, "Come on, Jacob, let's git y'ur mattress down from the loft an' carry it out ta my wagon ta make a place fer Alma Lee ta lie down on. It's a long, rough ride down ta Cove Mountain."

Jacob jerked his head around in surprise at what Hillard had said. "I figured we was a headin' ta the settlement!"

With a shake of his head, Hillard looked down at Jacob, gave a slight chuckle and said, "Boy, ya has got a lot ta learn. Us holler folks has always knowed it as the settlement, but it is rightly called Cove Mountain."

Hillard picked his hat up off the floor next to the wood stove and pushed it down tight on his head. "Let's git goin', Jacob. The road out of here is pretty rough, and I 'spect all of this cussed rain hain't done it any favors. We surely don't want ta be on it when it turns dark on us. Ya climb on up ta the loft an' hand me down y'ur mattress. I wants ta get it out ta the wagon afore the wind an' rain kick up some more."

Jacob scurried up the wooden rungs of the ladder and shoved his mattress over the edge to the big man below, who easily folded it in half and headed for the door.

Jacob slid down the side rails of the old ladder, just like he had been doing most of his life. He grabbed his coat and hat and headed out to give Hillard a hand stuffing the mattress into the wagon.

Once outside, Jacob could see that Hillard had come well prepared. Hillard had the tailgate down and was sliding the mattress into place. Jacob helped him tuck the last bit into place and asked, "What ya got in them feed sacks next ta the mattress?"

Hillard pulled the tarp he had strung over the entire wagon back in place to keep everything dry for Alma Lee. "I knowed what a rough ride it was goin' ta be, so I packed four of my old feed sacks full of hay. Onct we git y'ur sister in here, we can tuck them around her and keep her from bumpin' up agin the side of the wagon. That old, rough-sawn wood could be a might hard on her."

Jacob nodded in agreement. "Alma Lee is in enough pain an' I surely thank ya fer thinkin' about her comfort and all. I see ya got the tarp bowed up jest right so the rain runs down off both sides."

Hillard pulled the tarp up a bit higher and motioned for Jacob to take a look. "Ya see them wood slats I got runnin' from side ta side?

I built them in special fer when I hauls my lumber ta folks an' pack in supplies. I surely can't be gittin' my supplies all wet. I built this wagon nice an' tight outa my best white oak lumber, jest so no water can git in.

Hillard pulled the tarp back into place and put his hand on Jacob's shoulder. "Now let's git y'ur sister inta the wagon an' git goin'."

Inside the cabin, Granny had readied Alma Lee for her trip out of the hollow by wrapping her in her Maw's best quilt. She could hear Jacob and Hillard stomp on the porch, as they tried to rid their boots of the thick mud before entering the cabin.

The cabin door opened, and the two of them walked directly to the bed. Hillard gently scooped Alma Lee up and cradled her in his massive arms. She looked up at him with a thin smile. The moonshine was starting to do its job. He smiled back at her. "Don't ya be worryin' none, Alma Lee, we is goin' ta git ya some help."

Jacob grabbed Granny's slicker off the chair back and covered his sister with it, laid his hand lightly on her shoulder. I don't need ya ta be gittin' all wet before we git ya ta the wagon."

Granny spoke up. "I done give her a little swallow of the shine jest before ya come in. She should do jest fine till ya git her ta the settlement."

She handed the small jar of moonshine to Jacob. "Jest in case she needs another sip, or the two of ya feel a chill comin' on." She gave Hillard a sly wink.

Granny held the door open as Hillard carried Alma Lee out of the cabin and down the path to the waiting wagon. Jacob waited there with the tarp pulled up to make room for his sister. In one swift motion, Hillard placed Alma Lee onto the waiting mattress and tucked the feed sacks tightly around her.

Just before he closed the tailgate and pulled the tarp into place, Jacob leaned over and gave his sister a light kiss on the cheek. "Dontcha worry none Alma Lee," he whispered, "Everythin' is gonna be okay."

She let out a silly giggle and closed her eyes.

Jacob walked back to the porch, where Granny stood watching. He thanked her for what she had done. She gave him a reassuring hug. "The two of ya will be jest fine onct yer sister gits that operation. Ya will be back in the holler afore ya knowed it."

Jacob hurried down the path, climbed up onto the wet, wooden bench seat and hunkered down next to Hillard. He pulled his hat down tight, turned up the collar on his slicker, looked over at Hillard, and nodded. "She's all tucked in, let's git goin'."

Hillard slapped the reins to the back of the mules and they were on their way to Cove Mountain.

Cove Mountain wasn't a large town, as far as towns go. It had grown steadily over the years by folks who wanted more than the back-breaking way of life that hollow living gave them. The isolation up the hollows was more than some folks could take, and starting a town where the steep mountains opened up into a wide, fertile valley was more to their liking. To many, Cove Mountain was a gateway to the modern world, to a more civilized way of life.

Chapter 6

The old haul road leading out of the hollow started out rough and quickly got worse. True to Hillard's words, the weeks of hard rain had washed gullies in the mountain soil, exposing large rocks and boulders.

Jacob slammed into the side of the large man next to him, as one of the steel-rimmed wagon wheels crashed down off a large rock. "Hillard, how much more of this kinda punishment is we goin' ta have ta take? That last bump would have thrown me clean off of the wagon if ya hadn't been next ta me."

The words had no sooner cleared his lips as the wagon rounded a sharp bend in the storm-ravaged road. Hillard pulled back hard on the reins. "Whoa, mules." The wagon slid to a precarious stop as the mules and wagon broke over the crest of a steep downgrade. There before them lay a jumbled mass of rocks, boulders, broken trees and mounds of slick mountain mud. The landslide had wiped out most of the old road. Hillard let out a loud, "Whew!" He pulled back hard on the handbrake and wrapped the reins around it.

Jacob gripped the side of the wooden seat to keep from sliding off the wagon. "Man, Hillard, what are we goin' ta do now?"

Hillard looked to his left and then to his right. With a keen eye, he surveyed what was left of the road. He removed his stained felt hat, wiped the beads of sweat from his brow and spit a stream of tobacco juice over the side of the wagon. Hillard furrowed his brow as if he was in deep thought. "I don't rightly know, Jacob. I has ta think on it." He eased himself off the wagon into the deep mud and looked around to see what damage the slide had caused. With labored steps, he trudged alongside one of the mules talking in a soft tone as he patted the mule's back and cautiously worked his way forward.

At the mule's head he stopped. He dared not to make a false move on the slippery slope before him. The mule nuzzled him under the arm for attention. Hillard, never taking his eyes off of what used to be the road, reached over and scratched her between the ears as he methodically searched for a safe route through the maze of debris.

Jacob was about to jump down and join him, when the Hillard held up his hand. "Ya best stay right where ya is, Jacob. My mules jest might decide to git a closer look. Ya grab them reins jest in case."

Jacob loosened the reins from the brake handle and hollered over the howl of the wind, "It shore looks right dangerous ta me, Hillard. Do ya reckon we can git by?"

Hillard shielded his eyes against the downpour and took one last look at the tangled mass before him. He retraced his steps and hauled himself back aboard the wagon, all the while kicking the heavy mud from his boots. Taking the reins from Jacob, he gave him a worried look. "Whatever we does, we best git to it right quick." He nodded in the direction of the slope above them. "Take a look at them big trees up there. It looks like they's 'bout ready to join this big old mess any minute. I'm goin' ta git as close ta the edge of that ravine as I can. Ya best hang on real tight."

Jacob's face blanched as Hillard eased off the handbrake and guided the mules onto the slick mud-choked slope. Halfway down, the mules held their ground as the wagon started to slide closer to the edge of the ravine. Jacob scrambled to his right and latched onto the side of the slippery wooden seat. He watched in horror as Hillard clawed for a handhold. Jacob reached out and grabbed the collar of Hillard's jacket, just as the ground gave way under the back wheel nearest the edge of the ravine. The back corner of the wagon plunged down, burying the wheel and axle in the thick mud. The wagon tilted precariously. The mules brayed at the sudden strain and lunged into their harness in an effort to break the wagon free. Hillard stopped himself from being catapulted from the wagon by jamming his foot tight against the side of the wagon and yanked hard on the reins. "Whoa, mules. Ya hold on now, we hain't 'bout ta be goin' anyplace soon."

With the mules settled down, Hillard looked at Jacob. "Ya can let go of me now, Jacob. I thank ya fer keepin' me from goin' over the edge. It's a fur piece ta the bottom an' its plumb full of big old jagged rocks."

Jacob released his death grip and took a deep breath. "I hain't hardly been that scared in a long time, Hillard."

Hillard let out a nervous chuckle and slapped Jacob on the shoulder. "Ya best go check on Alma Lee, I'll git ta work on gittin' us outta here."

Without another word, Jacob vaulted over the side of the wagon and pulled himself along as he struggled toward the back of the wagon. He lowered the tailgate and loosened the tarp just enough to take a quick peek. With the wagon tilted at an odd angle, Alma Lee was held tight against the downhill bags of hay. She was still fast asleep.

Jacob retied the tarp and joined Hillard who was frantically dragging as many flat rocks as he could from the nearby piles of debris. Hillard gave him a weary look, steadied himself against the side of the wagon, took a deep breath and asked, "How is she, Jacob?"

Jacob looked at his friend who was now covered in mud. "She's doin' fine, as fer as I can tell. Now, what can I do ta git us outta here?"

Hillard grinned wide and reached out and wiped the slick mud from his hands on Jacob's pants and laughed.

Jacob screwed up his face and hollered, "Yuk! What'd ya do that fer?"

Hillard gave him an amused look. "I needs my hands somewhat clean so I can grab holt of the wagon. When I gits her up, ya can pack them rocks under the wheel until we's got it high enough ta drive outta here. Now git movin' afore this whole mountain side lets loose."

Jacob dug his boots in deep to keep from falling backwards into the ravine. He placed a large flat rock next to the wheel and watched as Hillard backed up to the wagon and took a firm grip on the undercarriage. Once he was set, he gave Jacob a nod, took a deep breath and let out a deep guttural groan as he lifted the wagon wheel and axle up out of the thick mud.

Jacob marveled at the strength of his friend as the sticky mud gave up its grip on the wheel with a loud sucking sound. Hillard's face flushed a bright crimson as the steely cords of his neck bulged.

With the wheel free and up about a foot, Jacob packed stone after stone in place as fast as humanly possible. With labored breath, Jacob packed one more rock under the wheel. When the rock slid into place, he hollered, "Let her down Hillard!"

Hillard blew out the breath he had been holding and collapsed against the side of the wagon. His arm draped over the top of the tarp, his massive chest heaved in and out as he sucked in the much needed fresh air. He looked to Jacob, who was still on his knees leaning against the wheel of the wagon, his head buried in his arms.

Hillard took one more deep breath and pushed himself away from the wagon. He reached out and patted Jacob on the head. "Ya did right good, Jacob. We has best git in the wagon afore another slide puts us over the edge." He offered Jacob a helping hand, which Jacob eagerly accepted.

Covered in mud from the waist down, they climbed aboard the wagon. Their strength sapped, they gave one another a half-hearted smile. Hillard released the brake and slapped the reins to the back of the mules. The mules leaned into their harness and strained against the pull of the wagon. The wagon lurched forward as the back wheel dropped off the pile of stones. Hillard guided the mules around several piles of debris, using the handbrake to keep the wagon from going into another slide.

After several harrowing minutes, they cleared the landslide and were back on firm ground.

Jacob turned and took one last look at the jumbled piles of debris they had negotiated. His shoulders sagged as he let out a sigh of relief, knowing they had narrowly escaped injury and possibly death.

Jacob turned to his friend, who stared straight ahead chewing his chaw of tobacco. "Hillard, I sure hope Alma Lee is doin' okay back there."

Hillard looked over at Jacob. "Ya jest hang on best ya can. The road levels off up ahead. Seein' as how the rain has let up some, we'll check on y'ur sister and give the mules a rest."

A quarter of a mile further, Hillard pulled the wagon to a stop.

The two climbed down, stretched their aching backs and walked to the back of the wagon to check on Alma Lee. Jacob untied the back of the tarp and lifted it up. Lying there, just as they had tucked her in back at the cabin, was Alma Lee sleeping soundly with a steady stream of soft snoring fluttering her lips.

Jacob looked over at Hillard with a contented smile. "She shore looks right comfortable back here an' not a drop of water ta be seen." He smiled again and replaced the tarp.

The sun broke through the heavy cloud cover briefly, just as they cleared the opening to the hollow. A wide open valley lay before them. The valley glistened as rays of sunlight bounced off the streams as they cascaded down the mountain slopes, headed for the swollen river that gleamed in the distance.

Jacob exhaled as he took in the beauty of the place. His eyes opened wider than ever and a look of awe spread across his youthful face like a wildfire out of control. He looked at Hillard, put his arm around the man's shoulder and gave it a strong squeeze. In a low wistful voice, said, "Man, Hillard, I hain't never seen such a sight in my life. Look how flat it is out there. It just goes on forever and ever."

Hillard looked at him. Jacob's pale blue eyes were misted with tears of joy. He knew they were tears of joy, because he had the same reaction the first time he looked out over the wide open valley some thirty odd years earlier. He clasped his hand on Jacob's shoulder and smiled knowingly, just as the clouds obscured the sun's rays and the rain, once again, began to fall.

Jacob smiled back and hunkered down next to Hillard, wondering what else awaited him in the outside world.

Two hours later, they approached the only river they must cross to get to the settlement, another eight miles further down the road.

Hillard hauled the mules to a stop and set the brake. He jumped down and walked over to the surging, swollen river. He looked up at Jacob and motioned for him to join him on the steep bank. Once there, Jacob let out a low whistle. "Hillard, do ya think we can git across safely?"

Hillard rubbed his day old stubble. He looked first up the river and then back down. "This here is the spot where I always has crossed an' I knowed it to be the most shallow. The mules an' my wagon are pretty heavy, so the current shouldn't cause us any problems, but I brought my big rope with me jest in case. I'm gonna tie the rope ta the back of the wagon an' wrap it around this here big, old tree. Ya can drive the team across an' I'll make sure the wagon don't start ta float downstream."

The color drained from Jacob's face. "Hillard, ya don't think the wagon will fill with water an' drown Alma Lee do ya?"

Hillard put his hand on Jacob's shoulder. "That wagon of mine is sealed so tight, it could be a boat. Don't ya be worryin' none. Alma Lee will be jest fine. Now, let's git to it afore the river rises any further."

Hillard peeled off his clothes, down to his shorts and walked over to the wagon. "Jacob, pull that box out from under the seat an' put my clothes in there. I'd rather be a might cold now as ta be soakin' wet an' miserable on the other side."

With the clothes stowed away for safekeeping, Jacob took a long look at the man who stood before him. Hillard was a mass of muscles and every time he moved, his muscles rippled under his hairy, well-tanned skin. Jacob was spellbound by the sheer size of the man. "Hillard, I don't believe I've ever seen so much muscle on one man an' so much hair ta boot."

Hillard grinned from ear to ear, as his round face flushed a bright red at Jacob's words. With a wave of his hand, he said, "Ya jest pay attention ta what ya is doin'." He let out a chuckle and picked up the end of the rope.

With Jacob in the driver's seat and the rope tied to the back of the wagon, Hillard wrapped the rope around the tree trunk several times. "Slap them reins ta the mules an' don't let up 'till the wagon clears the other bank."

Jacob took a deep breath and did as he was told. The mules lunged into the swollen stream. The cold water engulfed the mules, riding high on their backs. The wagon jolted down the steep, muddy bank into the river. The current caught the wagon and it began to float downstream. While the mules' shod-hooves clawed the river bed, Hillard strained against the pull of the wagon with all the strength he could muster. He slowly released his hold on the rope that snaked around the tree. The path of the wagon wasn't as straight as he wanted, but the mules were making headway and Jacob was hollering with all his might as the mules reached the far bank. After a few more adjustments of the rope, the mules hit solid ground, where their hooves dug in deep. The wagon lurched up over the crest of the bank and came to a sliding stop, as Jacob hauled back hard on the reins.

As the adrenaline coursed through his body, Jacob stood up in the wagon, pumped his fists skyward and let out a loud, "Yahoo!"

Hillard leaned against the tree. Drained of much of his strength, he smiled a tired smile and savored the enthusiasm of his young companion. He hollered out over the roar of the raging river. "Jacob, I'm gonna tie the rope around me an' ya can pull me across. It's kinda early fer my weekly bath, but I reckon it won't hurt none."

He let out a huge belly laugh, tied the rope securely around his massive waist and took off at a dead run toward the river, just as Jacob slapped the reins to the mules.

Safe on the other side of the river, Hillard stood next to the wagon shivering.

"Git them clothes of mine ya put in the box an' while ya's at it, pull out that poke of mine. I brung some clean clothes with me. Dig out a pair of shorts an' socks an' hand them on down."

Jacob hurried to comply. It didn't take Hillard long to throw on the dry clothes. He slapped himself all over to get his blood moving and climbed back up in the driver's seat. He looked over at Jacob and smiled. "Thank ya." He slapped the reins to the back of the mules and they were off once again toward the settlement.

Just as Hillard had said, the remaining road was considerably flatter. The downgrade gave the mules a much needed rest. Hillard and Jacob relaxed, lost in their own thoughts.

Now and then, Jacob would point out some distant landmark and Hillard would describe, as best he could, what they were seeing. Jacob's eyes roved from left to right and back again. He needed to draw in the immense view that lay before him and capture it securely in his memory. *Alma Lee has jest gotta hear all about this part of the trip ta the settlement.*

The sun peeked through the clouds several times and finally the rain stopped. As he looked out over the vast grasslands of the valley, interspersed with second-growth hardwoods, Jacob's thoughts turned to something his father had told him. He turned to Hillard. "Ya know what Paw used ta say 'bout the mountains an' the weather?" Hillard glanced in his direction. Jacob took it as a go ahead. "He said the mountains make their own weather. When the storm clouds come in, the mountain peaks jest reach up an' grab hold of them an' won't let go until they is wrung dry. I kinda guess that's why we's got some sunshine an' the rain has let up more an' more the further we gits away from the mountains."

Hillard looked over at him and grinned. "Y'ur paw was one smart man."

As the sun inched below the western horizon, muted hues of pink to light purple spread from the mountains across the open valley in a wash of silence, signaling the end of another day. As the last glimmer of daylight eased out of the valley, the wagon crested the last rise between the travelers and the settlement. Streetlights were blinking on. A warm glow emanated from the houses that lined the streets. A solitary automobile drove down one of the streets and pulled into a driveway. A sudden splash of red blazed bright as the car came to a stop.

Looking down on all of this, Jacob slowly released a faint gasp in awe of so many electric lights. A shiver ran down his back. "Would ya look at that, Hillard?" A wave of emotions surfaced, as Jacob's thoughts turned to his sister in the back of the wagon. *If only Alma Lee were awake, she would be amazed by the view from up here.*

Chapter 7

The coolness of the night air spread over the valley as the wagon reached the outskirts of Cove Mountain. Hillard coaxed the weary mules a little further down a graveled side road and pulled them up short in Cousin Mamie's driveway.

Mamie, Granny's cousin, sat knitting in her favorite chair. When she heard the gravel crunch under the wagon wheels and as Hillard called to his mules, she put her knitting aside. She flipped on the porch light and walked outside. Seeing her old friend, Hillard, sitting high up on his wagon, she hollered out, "Hillard, what in tarnation are you doin' down here this time of day? I haven't seen you in a long time. You best get down from there and give old Mamie a hug."

Jacob watched as Mamie stepped from her porch with a slight limp and walked toward the wagon. As she drew closer, he could see she was around Granny's age. Her gray hair was tied back in a bun. Her tan, wrinkled face with frameless spectacles perched on her generous nose mirrored the traits of Granny's family.

Hillard climbed down from the wagon, reached out and totally engulfed the little woman in one of his bear hugs. Jacob heard her laugh from someplace within Hillard's grasp, and then Hillard held her out at-arms-length and kissed her wrinkled cheek. He turned and gestured toward Jacob. "Mamie, this here is Jacob Holcomb from the holler. Jacob, git down from there and say hello ta Mamie."

Jacob lowered himself from the wagon and steadied himself until his tired legs could support him. Mamie looked up at him with a friendly grin and took his hand in hers. "Welcome to Cove Mountain, young man." She sized him up with an appreciative glance. "You are one handsome boy, and tall, too. How old are you, Jacob? What brings you to our little town?"

Jacob was thankful that Mamie's porch light wasn't too bright, because he could feel the color rising in his cheeks. He scuffed the gravel at his feet and managed to say, "Miz Mamie, I'm right close ta bein' sixteen. Granny had me come along ta help with my sister Alma Lee. She's in the back of the wagon. She's right sick. Granny says she has got ta git ta the hospital an' have an operation ta remove her appendix."

Hillard chimed in as he walked toward the back of the wagon. "Granny figured that ya could git her ta Fairmont in y'ur car."

Mamie looked up at Jacob with a concerned look. She laid her hand lightly on his shoulder. "Let me take a look at her, and don't you be worrying none. I will do whatever it takes to help your sister."

Walking toward the back of the wagon, she added, "Jacob, you can just plain call me Mamie. Everyone does."

Hillard had the tarp loosened and the tailgate down by the time Mamie got there. She reached in and laid her hand against Alma Lee's brow. With a "Tsk, tsk," she proclaimed, "This young lady is burnin' up somethin' fierce." With her hands planted firmly on her hips, she looked first at Hillard and then Jacob. "What in the world did Granny give her? She smells like she's been drinkin' hard licker."

Jacob began to explain, the best he could. "My sister was in a whole heap of pain, an' Granny had me fetch some of Tollivar Hicks' shine ta help ease her misery. It seemed ta work jest fine, 'cause she slept all the way here."

Mamie knew all about the healing properties of old Tollivar's moonshine. With a clever smile, she chuckled and shook her head. "Tollivar has been healin' a whole bunch of folks here about for years and years. Some that is sick, and then there are those that just plain likes the stuff." She laughed heartily.

Her expression suddenly turned serious. Mamie looked directly at the two of them. "Now, let's get your sister out of the wagon and into the back seat of that old car of mine. The hospital in Fairmont is over twenty miles from here. We have got to get her there before this shine wears off."

Hillard lifted Alma Lee gingerly from the wagon and walked with her toward the waiting car, "I don't recall ever seein' you or your sister in Cove Mountain before, Jacob."

Before answering, Jacob watched as Hillard carefully place his sister in the backseat of the car. "This here is the first time that either of us has ever left the holler. It shore is a lot different than where we live."

Mamie slowly released her breath, her brow wrinkled. "I've seen several of you Winder Holler folks come to the settlement for the first time. It can be a shock for some, and there are those that have a right hard time adjustin' to the outside way of life. Fairmont is a whole heap bigger than this place and that surely can be a big problem."

Hillard made Alma Lee as comfortable as possible in the back seat, covered her with the quilt, and shut the car door. Mamie slapped the trunk lid with the flat of her hand. "The time for talking is over. I'll grab my purse and car keys from the house and be on my way to the hospital. The two of you can make yourselves comfortable here at my place until I bring Alma Lee back. Hopefully, it won't take the doctors long to figure out what's wrong with her and get her back on the mend."

Mamie hurried to the house as Hillard ruffled Jacob's thick, light brown hair. "I told ya that everythin' was goin' ta be ok. Mamie will see ta it that y'ur sister gits the help she needs."

As Mamie came out of the house and headed for the car, Hillard told Jacob, "Ya best go grab that poke with y'ur sister's clothes in it an' put it in the front seat."

Mamie started the car and buckled up tight. She looked over her shoulder at her sleeping passenger, said a silent prayer, and backed her car out of the drive. With a wave of her hand, she pressed down on the gas, kicking up some loose gravel and sped off down the road towards the hospital.

Hillard and Jacob stood in the middle of the road and watched Mamie drive away. The red glow of the taillights disappeared into the darkness.

Hillard watched Jacob staring wistfully at the star littered sky. Jacob spotted him out of the corner of his eye. "Would ya look at the beauty of all this shinin' down on us, Hillard," he said softly. "I hain't seen so many stars in all my life."

Hillard spoke up, "Yep, I knowed exactly what ya mean. It kinda gits to a body and makes ya git ta thinkin'."

The mules stomped their feet, shook their large heads and snorted.

"Sounds like my mules is gettin' restless. Come on Jacob, let's git ya settled inside. I has ta take my wagon and mules over ta the neighbor's barn and git them fed an' settled down fer the night. I'll git back quick as I can. An' when I git here, I'll try an' answer all of the questions ya surely must have."

Chapter 8

To drive the narrow, winding road to Fairmont was demanding. Come nighttime it could be deadly. Mamie knew she couldn't waste time getting Alma Lee to the hospital, but to drive too fast would surely get them in an accident. Not only were the deer thick on the roads at night, but navigating the snake-like curves along the steep mountain road would take all the concentration she could muster.

In her rush to get Alma Lee to the hospital, Mamie sailed around a sharp curve too fast and ran off the edge of the pavement. The sudden drop-off startled her. Pulling hard on the wheel and easing off of the gas, she managed to bring the old car safely back onto the blacktop. She loosened her death grip on the steering wheel and slowed the car to a crawl. She peered in here rearview mirror to see if Alma Lee was okay. To here relief, Alma Lee was still lying on the backseat sound asleep.

Once her heart quit pounding, she took a deep breath, adjusted herself comfortably in the old, worn seat and slowly accelerated.

The drive settled into a more sensible pace as Mamie softly hummed her favorite tune. The miles rolled pleasantly by.

Rounding a sharp curve, she spotted a small herd of deer in a roadside meadow. Their heads jerked up as one, and they stared into the bright headlights. She eased off on the accelerator and mumbled to herself, "Just keep your eyes peeled, you old fool, and get ready to slam on the brakes if they decide to bolt across the road." To her relief, they didn't twitch a muscle and she sailed on by with no problem. Only then did she slowly release the breath she unknowingly held back.

Mamie was totally exhausted from the long harrowing drive, when she topped the ridge of the last mountain between her and Fairmont. The city spread out over the valley below. The sparkle of the city lights against the coal black sky, cast a magical spell upon the landscape. She watched as headlights silently negotiated the sweeping curves of the road far below. The road followed the path of the Monogahela River, as it journeyed through the center of town.

Mamie was jolted out of her reverie by a sudden movement and a low moan from the back seat. Her dread of Alma Lee waking from her drunken stupor was now a reality. She accelerated hard and the car rose to the challenge, speeding faster and faster down the winding road. Every now and then, Mamie glanced in her rearview mirror to check on her passenger. She detected no more movement in the backseat. In a deep, soulful voice, Mamie prayed, "Oh Lord, please don't let this child wake up before I get her to the hospital."

Mamie had passed one car after another. With the hospital in sight, and only a quarter-of-a-mile to go, Alma Lee, suddenly and without warning, bolted upright and let out a piercing scream.

Her senses jolted by the sudden outburst, Mamie turned in her seat to check on Alma Lee and almost sideswiped a parked car. Alma Lee's rambling, incoherent words made it impossible for Mamie to understand anything she was saying. With the car slowed and under control, Mamie finally heard her mumble, in between sobs of despair, "Jacob, where are ya at, brother? I don't know where I is, an' this thing I'm in is goin' as fast as the wind blows. Lord! Where has ya delivered me ta? The bright lights, they hurt my eyes, an' they is everywhere I look. Jacob, ya has got ta come help me."

Mamie gathered her wits about her and talked to Alma Lee in a soft, controlled voice. "Alma Lee, honey, I'm Granny's cousin from the settlement. I'm taking you to the hospital where the doctors are going to make you all better. I know this here city is a lot for you to take all at once, but if you'll just cover your head with your maw's quilt, things won't seem so strange."

Mamie wiped her sweaty palms on her dress, took a deep breath and continued. "We are just now getting into the emergency area of the hospital. I'll stay with you all of the time you're here." Those reassuring words reduced Alma Lee's outburst to low plaintive sobbing and incoherent mumbling.

When the car stopped at the entrance to the emergency room, Mamie laid on the horn until the emergency nurse and an aide exited the hospital and rushed to the car.

Mamie opened the rear door. The nurse leaned into the car. There, huddled in the far corner, was Alma Lee, her knees tucked tightly against her chest, and a flushed face dripping with sweat. She sat there clutching the quilt in both hands, her lower lip quivering as her eyes darted wildly about, a look of total bewilderment etched upon her face.

The nurse assessed the situation quickly. The distraught, young woman before her was in dire need of a sedative. She snapped out an order to the aide, "Get a wheelchair. We have to get this young lady into the emergency room now."

Mamie talked calmly to Alma Lee, as the three of them coaxed her from the backseat of the car. Mamie held Alma Lee's hand as a constant reassurance that she would be okay, Alma Lee reluctantly collapsed into the wheelchair.

In the emergency room, Alma Lee lay on the table holding Mamie's hand. Her eyes roamed warily about the room. "The doctor will be here real soon, child," she said, hoping to relieve some of Alma Lee's anxiety.

The doctor entered the room and approached the examining table. "What seems to be the problem, nurse?"

"We have a probable case of appendicitis and as you can see, this young woman is very distraught. She needs a sedative, but the exam has to be done first."

He nodded in agreement and looked at Mamie. "And you are a relative of hers?"

Mamie held out her hand. "You can call me Mamie. I'm a cousin of Granny Harris. She's the one who knew Alma Lee was a needin' an operation. Granny had Hillard bring her out of the holler to my place in Cove Mountain. I put her in my car and drove her here. She shore is sick and frightful for bein' out of the holler. Is she goin' to be okay?"

He patted her hand lightly in assurance. "I believe we can make her better, but first I must examine her."

He leaned forward, laid his hand gently on Alma Lee's shoulder, looked her in the eye and smiled. "Young lady, I'm Dr. Lane and I have to push on your abdomen a little to find out what the problem is. I promise I'll be as gentle as I can."

Alma Lee looked up at him and weakly muttered, "Ya go ahead, doctor, but I knowed it's gonna hurt somethin' fierce."

He probed as gently as he could. It was obvious what was wrong with her as she sucked in air and her face contorted with pain.

The doctor looked from Alma Lee to Mamie, shaking his head. "I'm afraid your Granny Harris was right. You do have appendicitis. We will have to operate as soon as possible."

Alma Lee jerked her head around and stared directly at Mamie, the look of sheer panic confronted, Mamie. Fearing another bout of hysteria, Mamie pleaded with the doctor. "Can you give her something to calm her down, Doctor?" He nodded his head. "We have the sedative ready. I had to wait until I completed the examination before we could give it to her."

Mamie let out a weary sigh of relief as the nurse gave Alma Lee the shot.

Dr. Lane turned to the aide. "We've got to get her to the operating room stat. Nurse, would you show Miz Mamie to the waiting room?"

As the aide rolled Alma Lee from the emergency room, the doctor leaned over, held her hand and in a gentle voice, said, "Miz Alma Lee, you are going to be just fine."

She looked up at him with a lopsided grin. In a soft slurred voice, she managed to say, "Ya sure do have purtty hair." Then she giggled.

He smiled back. "And you too have beautiful, red hair." He squeezed her hand gently as they entered the elevator.

Dr. Lane, clad in his green scrubs and his mask hanging loosely around his neck, walked into the waiting room. He spotted Mamie sitting in a comfortable chair her head bent low, eyes closed and her glasses down on the end of her nose. He walked over and placed his hand on her shoulder and gave it a slight shake, "Miz Mamie."

Mamie's eyes fluttered open and she jerked her head back. She placed her hand on her chest and laughed nervously. "Lord! Doctor, you scared the daylights out of me."

He sat down next to her. Feeling a little foolish for scaring her, he said, "I truly didn't mean to scare you so, but I was eager to let you know how Miz Alma Lee is doing. She came through the operation just fine. It's a good thing you got her here when you did. Her appendix had ruptured and without the operation, she may not have survived."

Mamie sat forward in the chair, rubbed her hands together nervously and asked, "Is she going to be stayin' here a long time because of that?"

He reached over and took her hands in his. "She's going to be okay. We may have to keep her here a few extra days, but she's young and she'll heal quickly." Mamie breathed a sigh of relief and nestled back into the comfort of the chair. He continued, "I have several questions concerning Miz Alma Lee. Are you up to answering them?"

She smiled, "You just go right ahead and ask. I'll try and help you as much as I can."

"First off, I didn't get a chance to properly introduce myself. I'm Dr. Lane. I've been here for a little over six months. And I've seen a lot of patients come through the doors since then, but Miz Alma Lee is the first one with such a smell of alcohol about her."

Mamie chuckled and slapped her knee. "That's 'cause Granny Harris, the Healer, was the one to give her the shine to help with the pain she was havin'. Granny has lots of natural potions and the like, but she don't have nothin' stronger than shine to help the poor souls who needs some relief from their misery. Remember, I told you Granny Harris was the one to know Alma Lee was a needin' an operation and that's why I brought her here. I don't know what more I can tell you, because I met the young lady not more than four hours ago at my place in Cove Mountain."

"So, that's where she's from?"

"Oh no, Alma Lee is from Winder Holler, way back up in the mountains. Accordin' to her brother, Jacob, she's nineteen and neither of them has ever been out of the holler."

"So, you're telling me this young lady has never been to Cove Mountain, let alone Fairmont?"

She shrugged her shoulders. "That's what I'm tellin' you."

He sat back and rubbed his chin considering all he'd been told. "Are you going to be staying here until Alma Lee is released? If you are, I sure would like to find out a little more about this Granny Harris and Winder Hollow."

"I was plannin' on stayin' with her. . . but, Doctor, when will I be able to see Alma Lee? I do believe she is goin' to be needin' me close by when she wakes up. I'm afraid her bein' in this strange place will be right hard for her to understand. You just might have to give her more of that medicine to keep her calmed down."

A knowing smile crossed his face. "Don't you worry. I have already written the order to keep her sedated. I'll be looking in on her for the rest of the night. By the way, there's a spare bed in Miz Alma Lee's room. You are welcome to use it. I'll have the aid take you to her room. You look as if you could use a good night's sleep." He patted her hand, smiled and walked out of the room.

Once the aide had left, Mamie removed her dress, placed it over a chair, kicked off her slippers and put her glasses on the bedside stand. She crawled between the crisp, white sheets and closed her eyes. The day had been long and tiring. She fell fast asleep.

Mamie sat bolt upright her heart pounding. A loud moan from Alma Lee had awakened her. "Where am I?" Alma Lee said weakly. "An' who are ya?"

Mamie pulled back the covers, swung her legs over the edge of the bed and stood on wobbly legs. She stretched her sore body, shuffled over to Alma Lee and reached out and touched her hand, lightly. "I'm Granny Harris's cousin, Mamie. I'm the one who brought you to the hospital. Thank God you slept most of the way here. We didn't have much time to get acquainted, 'cause I was driving like a crazy fool down them darn mountain roads.

As far as where you're at, this is the hospital in the city of Fairmont. Dr. Lane had to operate on you to remove your appendix. That's what all your pain was about."

While Mamie talked, Alma Lee looked timidly around the room. It was full of strange things she had never seen before. It had an entirely different smell to it and the walls were bright and shiny. She spotted the black box on the wall above Mamie's head and pointed at it. "What in tarnation is that thing?"

Mamie gave the box a quizzical look. "I don't rightly know, but I do believe it could be what they call a television. I don't have such a thing back in Cove Mountain, but I've heard of them. Maybe in the mornin' we can get someone to show us how it works, but right now you have got to get some rest. I'll do my best to help you understand all 'bout your new surroundin's, come mornin'."

Mamie, still bone weary from the long day, returned to her bed and promptly fell fast asleep.

Alma Lee was not so lucky. Sleep evaded her. Still groggy from the sedative, she couldn't decipher the strange sounds that seemed to surround her.

The noises made by people as they walked up and down the hallway, the constant calls over the paging system and the shrill sound of the ambulance siren, as it pulled up to the hospital, were more than she could comprehend.

The first time she heard voices over the paging system, she thought it had to be a ghost trying to contact her from the nether world. Her heart beat rapidly as a wave of anxiety washed over her over. Looking wildly about, she spotted the I.V. tube running from the plastic bag above her into her arm. She raised her other arm in an effort to remove the tube and felt the tug of the wire that was hooked to her finger. The blood pressure cuff around her arm was more than she could comprehend. She choked back a scream and remained riveted to the bed, trembling and silently repeated, *I needs ta git back ta Winder Holler, an' I wants ta see Jacob. Oh Lord! Please git me outta here.*

Chapter 9

Back at Cove Mountain, Jacob and Hillard talked into the wee hours of the morning about their trip to the settlement and their concern for Alma Lee.

Because Mamie did not surround herself with many modern conveniences, Jacob had a much easier time than Alma Lee, adjusting to the outside world. He was amazed with what electricity could do for you and the inside plumbing with running water was a marvel. The flush toilet seemed like a strange thing to have right inside your own home.

Hillard had a tough time explaining some of these modern conveniences to Jacob, and several sips from the moonshine jar didn't help matters.

He looked at Jacob with bloodshot eyes. In a slurred voice, he said, "We'd best git us some shut-eye, Jacob. I plan on showin' ya 'round Cove Mountain come daylight, an' I 'spect ya could use some sleep y'urself." On unsteady legs, Hillard showed Jacob where the bedroom was and with a big, goofy grin on his flushed face, said, "Ya are really goin' ta like this bed," and staggered out.

Once Hillard was gone, Jacob removed his clothes, sat on the edge of the bed, bounced up and down a couple of times, and in one easy motion, swung his legs over the edge and lay down. He rested his head on the soft pillow and immediately felt like he had died and gone to Heaven. This would be his first time ever sleeping on an innerspring mattress. He settled into the comfort of the bed. A broad smile spread across his face and he was fast asleep.

Chapter 10

The first rays of sunlight filtered through the hospital window as Alma Lee opened her eyes to a place she had only a vague memory of. The sedative had worn off, only adding to her confusion. Her first thought was to jump out of bed and run as fast as her legs could carry her. But a warm, rugged hand gently wrapped around her own and Mamie spoke softly, "Child, you just lay back and let your head clear a bit. Old Mamie will try and fill you in on all of them blank spots you surely must have." Mamie leaned back in the chair with a consoling smile and waited for her words to sink in.

Alma Lee felt much better with the warm hand holding hers, but she couldn't shake the nervousness she felt as she curiously surveyed the room. The strange sounds of the hospital only added to her confusion.

Tears flowed down her cheeks in salty streams. "Mamie, I knowed ya done me right by bringin' me here last night, but this here place is 'bout ready ta make me jump plumb outta my skin." She swiped at the tears with the back of her hand. "Please, Mamie, when can I git outta here an' git back ta my cabin in Winder Holler?"

Mamie leaned forward and was about to speak, when the door opened and Dr. Lane walked in. Alma Lee quickly wiped the tears from her eyes and cheeks with the sheet. Dr. Lane was slight of build and looked to be in his early thirties. He had light reddish hair, cut short. There was something familiar about his hair, but she couldn't quite remember what it was.

With a friendly smile, he walked over to her and introduced himself. "Miz Alma Lee, I'm Dr. Lane. I'm the doctor who took out your appendix. I hope you are feeling much better." He reached over, took her hand and with a gentle, reassuring squeeze, tilted his head slightly and said, "I understand this is your first time in Fairmont and it's a great shock to you. I hope you will trust me to see that you get the best care we have to offer. Your quick recovery is my main concern. Once we have taken care of that, Miz Mamie can return you to your home in the hollow. I might add that you are very fortunate to have a good friend like Miz Mamie, who got you to the hospital in the nick of time. You were one sick young lady."

As she looked into his eyes, Alma Lee could see his sincerity. His voice was very soothing. Any apprehension she felt melted away. "I surely do thank ya fer what ya done fer me, but can ya tell me when I can git back home?"

He looked at her with a knowing smile. "We'll do our best to get you out of here in a couple of days. Miz Mamie will be staying with you until it's time for you to be released. So, just lie back and relax. I will check in on you later in the day. The staff will be bringing breakfast for the two of you in a few minutes. In the meantime, why not watch some television?"

Mamie gave him an odd look. "Dr. Lane, I don't have no television at my place in Cove Mountain. Alma Lee, livin 'back in Winder Holler, don't have electricity, telephone, running water, or any such modern things. The people who live in the holler are the hardest workin', self-providin' bunch of folks you would ever want to meet. They don't hold much truck with the outside way of life. They are a proud people who like their privacy. Alma Lee was born there, and as I told you, up until now, has never left it. Now, how do you expect either of us to know anythin' 'bout a television?"

He picked up the remote and pushed the "on" button. The color picture that flashed before their eyes totally amazed them. Alma Lee watched wide-eyed, doubting her senses. *How did they git those small people inta that black box?*

Dr. Lane could see the confusion on their faces, as they craned their necks to get a better look. He began to explain how a television works. "I know what I'm about to say will be hard to understand, but I'll try my best to keep it simple. There is a thing called a camera that takes a picture of things. The camera can project, or show, what it sees into the box we call a television. Here, let me show you how it works." He handed the remote to Mamie and showed her which buttons to push to change channels and the ones to raise or lower the volume. Mamie and Alma Lee sat there in awe, their mouths hanging wide open.

Alma Lee finally spoke up. "Would ya look there, Mamie? I hain't never seen such a thing in my life. Push that changin' button again."

Dr. Lane walked from the room smiling, shaking his head. The sound of their voices followed him down the hallway as they laughed and carried on like a couple of school girls.

Chapter 11

Jacob woke to the smell of fresh brewed coffee and bacon frying in the skillet. Hillard was talking to himself, as Jacob stuck his head around the corner. "Man! Hillard, that shore do smell good. I believe I could eat a whole slab of that bacon this mornin'."

Hillard gave a slight chuckle. "Ya jest set y'urself down ta the table, an' I'll scramble up a bunch of these here eggs ta go with the bacon. Ya can help y'urself ta the coffee. Ya best set y'urself down and fill up on this grub, 'cause I has a whole heap of things ta show ya today. We can git goin' right after we take care of my mules."

Like most young boys, Jacob didn't have to be told twice about eating. He attacked the food as if he hadn't eaten in weeks. He could hardly wait to see all the things in Cove Mountain that Hillard had told him about.

With the mules fed and watered, Jacob and Hillard took their time as they walked the gravel roads. They'd walked but a short block when Jacob spotted a shiny, red car parked in one of the driveways. He looked it over appreciatively. "Hillard, has ya ever taken a ride in one of them contraptions?"

Hillard laughed heartily, "I did onct, an' it scared me ta death. I like the slow, easy pace of my mules a heap better."

Jacob snickered and gave him a good-natured shove as they continued down the street. Jacob pointed out everything of interest along the way.

Downtown was a collection of miscellaneous stores. The small post office was in the center of town, with the other businesses scattered here and there along the main street. There was a steady stream of people going in and out of most buildings, but one in particular had more than the rest.

"How come so many folks is goin' inta that there buildin'?" asked Jacob.

Hillard took him by the arm. "Ya jest foller me an' ya can see fer y'urself."

Jacob stared wide-eyed as they walked through the door. Finally, he managed to say, "I haint never seen so much store-bought food in my whole life."

Hillard laughed and put his hand on Jacobs shoulder. "Boy, where did ya think all of the sugar, coffee, flour an' the likes that we eat comes from? We do right well up the holler providin' fer ourselves, but there is a whole heap of things we needs jest ta git by. I haul a bunch of stuff outta the holler these folks can use, an' in turn, I bring stuff back what we be needin'."

Jacob caught the drift of what Hillard was saying. He nodded his head as Hillard's words sunk in. "I never give it much thought as ta what happened ta all the stuff Maw and Paw growed an' made, but it shore do make sense now."

This was the first time Hillard had heard him mention his folks. In a consoling voice, he asked, "How long has it been, Jacob, since the bad accident took y'ur maw an' paw?"

The memory of the accident was still vivid in Jacob's mind, but he hadn't talked about it in a very long time. He stuck his hands in his pants pockets, looked down at the floor, and in a disheartened tone, said, "Hillard, it's right hard ta talk 'bout, but I 'spect it's goin' on 'bout three years now." When he looked up, Hillard could see the distant look in Jacob's eyes. Jacob looked about the store, choked back the tears and continued. "I can still remember the day when the three of us was up agin the mountain side cuttin' firewood. Paw was cuttin' down a big, old dead tree. It fell inta another one an' got hung up. Paw was startin' ta cut the other tree when a big wind came up an' got the dead tree ta fallin'. Maw was carryin' some small pieces of wood ta the wagon an' didn't see the tree a headin' her way. Paw took off runnin' ta push her out of the way, an' the tree fell on ta both of em. It killed 'em both, right on the spot."

Jacob snuffed a couple of times and wiped his nose with his sleeve. "I still have powerful bad dreams 'bout it, an' I don't like ta talk 'bout it much."

Hillard knew he had opened up an old wound and was sorry he'd even asked the question. He quickly changed the subject. "Come on, Jacob, let me show ya 'round a bit more, an' I'll treat ya ta y'ur first meal at the little restaurant they has down the street. They serve food a whole heap better than I can cook. I bet we can git them ta dig up some soup beans an' cornbread. It shore oughta make ya feel better."

Jacob grinned wide. "Hillard, ya knowed it's my favorite kinda food. What are we waitin' fer?"

The sun was high in the sky when they emerged from the restaurant. Jacob wiped his mouth with the back of his hand. "Man, Hillard, that was some of the best soup beans I has ever ate. Did ya see the size of that piece of apple pie she put on my plate?"

Hillard chuckled. "I did, an' it was a joy ta watch ya dig inta it. Ya keep eatin' that way, an' ya jest might git as big as me." Hillard slapped him on the back and laughed. "Come on, Jacob, I've got ta check in at the post office an' the feed store over there."

When Hillard opened the door to the post office, the clerk, who had been sorting the day's mail, looked up.

"Hillard, what are you doing here? I thought you weren't coming back for another week."

Hillard walked to the caged opening and leaned his elbows on the counter, blocking Jacob's view of the woman. Hillard removed his hat and set it on the counter and hooked a thumb over his shoulder toward Jacob. "I had ta make an emergency trip ta bring this young feller's sister ta Mamie's place. She's right sick, an' Mamie has taken her ta the hospital in Fairmont."

The woman stood on her tiptoes and peered over Hillard's shoulder. "Howdy, young man, what's your name?"

Jacob stuffed both hands in his pockets and flashed the woman his biggest smile. "I'm Jacob Holcomb, Ma'am."

She smiled back at him. "You wouldn't be related to Winfred and Grace Holcomb, would you?"

Jacob's ears perked up at the mention of his maw and paw's names. "Yes I am, Ma'am. They is my maw and paw. . ." his voice trailed off as he shifted uncomfortably from one foot to the other.

The woman, sensing his discomfort about her question, offered her condolence. "I was very sad to hear of their passing. They were such nice people. I'm truly sorry for your loss." She set the bundle of mail she was sorting on the counter. "They didn't come to town very often, but when they did, Grace would always bring me a jar of her homemade blackberry jam. She would always say it was their way of thanking me for seeing that the mail got to Winder Hollow with as little delay as possible. I do miss your maw's jam and pleasant conversations."

Hillard stood silently watching his young friend's reaction to the lady's words. He knew that Jacob would shake off the memory of his maw and paw's death, just as he had earlier in the day. Hillard decided it was time to move on. He turned to the woman. "I should be headin' back ta the holler in a day or two. I'll stop back in an' git what mail ya has ready ta go."

"I'll have it ready whenever you are," she said, with a smile. She returned to her mail sorting and as an after thought, added, "Say 'Hi' to Emily for me, Hillard."

Hillard smiled. "I shore will."

"Come on, Jacob," Hillard said, as he started for the door, "I want ta show ya the feed store."

Before Jacob made it to the door, the clerk hollered out, "I hope your sister gets to feeling better, young man."

Jacob turned and waved. "Thank ya, Ma'am. I hope she gits better real soon, too."

The feed store was a short block away. Hillard and Jacob walked along the edge of the graveled street to take advantage of the shade from the large trees that lined the street. Every now and then, someone would holler out to Hillard and he would wave one of his large hands and call out a "Howdy" to them.

Jacob kicked a stone that lay in his path and looked up at his friend. "Ya shore do know a heap of people here in the settlement."

Hillard chuckled. "I guess ya could say that. I make the trip outta the holler 'bout twice a month ta git the mail, pick up supplies and deliver a load of lumber. Emily comes with me now-and-then when she needs ta git some material from the general store. It shore do make the trip more interestin, an' not nearly as lonely."

"I see what ya mean," Jacob said, as he kicked another stone. He watched it tumble down the street and skid to a stop. "It's a right nice trip, but havin' company is a comfort ta most."

Hillard grinned. "It shore is."

They turned the corner and Hillard pointed down the street at a large clapboard building. "There she is, Jacob. The feed and supply store." The man hooked an arm around Jacob's shoulder, gave him a good squeeze. "Come on, Jacob, ya is really goin' ta like lookin' 'round in there."

Jacob placed both hands on his hips, rocked back on his heels and let out a low whistle as he entered the building. His eyes roamed from left to right as he took in the row after row of stocked shelves, heavy with all kinds of hardware. Off to his left, he spotted a display of new chainsaws of every size and color. The bright lights made them dazzle before his eyes. "Man, Hillard, would ya look over there. I never seen so many saws in my life." If Hillard answered, Jacob didn't hear him. He made a beeline to the display and ran his hands over the smooth housings of the saws. He chose one and lifted it from the display stump it was sitting on. A wide grin formed at the corners of his mouth as he turned to Hillard. "Haint she a beauty, Hillard? This here saw is the lightest one I has ever latched on ta. It shore beats the one I has at home."

Hillard gave the saw an appreciative look. "That's the one I've had my eye on for sometime now. It's one of them new German saws, made by the Stihl Company. I need me one more big order for wood, and that saw will be mine. Talking 'bout wood, you go ahead an' look around. I'm gonna talk ta the owner an' see if he needs more."

Hillard had no sooner headed for the sales counter, when Jacob spotted a display of leather work boots at the far end of the store. He checked out all the racks of shiny new axes, shovels and hoes along the way. Just before he reached the shoes, he came upon a wire rack full of seed packets. The colorful pictures of the flowers drew his attention. Gazing from one packet to another, he spotted many of the flowers he knew and some he had never laid eyes on. Several caught his eye and he pulled them from the rack. His first thoughts were of Alma Lee. *I think these here flowers would really look good in Alma Lee's flower beds. She shore does like her flowers.*

The smell of new leather tempted Jacob to stop and look over the display of boots, but now he was on a mission for his ailing sister.

Finding Hillard with the store owner, he waited until they stopped talking. Hillard gave him a sideways glance. A smile lit up his face as he spotted the seed packets clutched in Jacob's hand. "Whatcha got there, Jacob?"

Jacob fanned out the three packets like a deck of cards and held them up for Hillard to see. "I kinda figured that these flower seeds might boost Alma Lee's spirits when she gits back from the hospital. Only thing is. . . I done left the holler without a cent ta my name. They is thirty-five cents a pack an' I would need a little over a dollar ta buy them. Do ya have any money on ya? I'll pay ya back as soon as we git back ta the holler. Honest! Whatcha think, Hillard?"

Hillard turned to the store owner and winked. "I 'spect I could float ya a loan fer a few days."

Jacob quickly laid the prized seed packets on the counter. He watched as Hillard paid the man and the seed packets disappeared into a small paper sack. With the bag held tightly in his hand, he turned to his friend, eyes glistening with pride. "Thank ya, Hillard. Alma Lee is really goin' ta like this present. I 'spect she will find just the right spot ta plant them."

Hillard chuckled. "I 'spect she will, Jacob." He then turned to the store owner, shook his hand. "I want ta thank ya fer the lumber order. I'll have it ta ya next week."

The man turned to Jacob. "Young man, I hope your sister likes the gift. And, Hillard, next week sounds fine for delivering the lumber. I'll be looking for you."

Hillard turned and headed for the door. "Come on, Jacob, we best head back ta the house. We'll take a different way back so ya can see more of the town."

Two blocks from the downtown area, they came to the community school. As they got closer, they heard a chorus of laughter and hollering coming from the far side of the building. Jacob looked at Hillard. "It shore sounds like someone is havin' fun."

In a nearby field, a group of young boys were playing football. Hillard and Jacob watched as the ball was snapped to a tall, slender boy standing twenty feet back from the lineman in front of him. The opposing team made a mad rush toward the blockers, screaming and hollering as they hit head on in an attempt to break through the line. Most were held in check or dumped to the ground in a maze of tangled arms and legs. Jacob pointed to one boy at the far end of the scrimmage line. "Look there, Hillard! That feller's fast."

The boy had knocked his blocker to the ground, and in a blaze of speed, was bearing down on the kicker. He was three short strides from reaching his foe, when the tall boy took one quick step forward, his leg came up and his foot caught the ball perfectly with a, sharp resounding thump. All eyes watched as the ball soared, as in slow motion, over the heads of the tangle of players and the two receivers who had hoped to catch the ball and run it back. Jacob watched wide-eyed as the ball hit the ground beyond the playing field. It tumbled end-over-end and came to rest at his feet.

"Hey, fella, could you toss us the ball?", asked the kicker.

Jacob reached down and picked it up. He juggled it from hand-to-hand, just to get the feel of it. In one quick and easy motion, he took one step forward and let the ball fly. The perfect spiral of the football sailed over the two receivers, the now-standing clutch of linesmen and the waiting hands of the kicker. All eyes watched as the ball hit the ground ten yards beyond the tall boy. A chorus of cheers, laughter and a few "wows!" were heard from the dumb-founded players. "That was one wicked sixty-yard pass. Where are you from, fella?", asked one of the players.

"I'm jest visitin' from Winder Holler," Jacob answered.

The boy smiled wide. "Well, holler boy, you can come play with us anytime you get to town." He waved and trotted back toward the other players.

Jacob waved back. "I shore will."

Hillard's eyes were still wide with amazement as Jacob walked back to where he stood. He clapped a hand to Jacob's shoulder. "That shore was one amazin' throw, Jacob. I'm right proud of ya. I had no idea ya was gittin' that strong."

Jacob beamed brightly at his friends praise. "I hain't nearly strong as ya are Hillard, but I is workin' on it."

Hillard chuckled, "Well, holler boy, how's 'bout ya give me a hand back at the barn. One of my mules has a slight limp an' I needs ta check it out."

The din emanating from the football field grew faint after the first block. Jacob turned and took one last lingering, look at the field of players. He couldn't help but wonder. *Could that be me playing with them boys, if Maw and Paw were still alive?* A smile tugged at the corner of his mouth, as he hurried to catch up with Hillard.

Chapter 12

Dr. Lane walked into the room. Both women were sound asleep with the television still on. He reached over and pushed the "off" button. Alma Lee's eyes fluttered open. She stretched, gave a big yawn and, in a sleepy voice, said, "What did ya do that fer doctor? I was jest gitt'n used ta how that there thing worked."

He smiled. "You'll have plenty of time to watch it later, but if you don't mind, could we talk about the Healer woman who sent you here?"

Alma Lee eased herself into a comfortable sitting position, adjusted her hospital gown, and looked him in the eye. "What is it ya want ta know 'bout Granny?"

He wrinkled his brow in deep thought. "Miz Mamie was telling me all about how she does the healing of the folks who live in Winder Hollow. I'm very interested in the old-time remedies the mountain people use. I'm also amazed that she figured out what your problem was and that she knew it was a very serious condition. I'd really like to meet her someday." He shifted his weigh from one foot to the other. He hesitated a moment. "Do you mind if I sit on the bed for a minute or two?"

Alma Lee patted the bed and smiled. "Dr. Lane, ya just set y'urself down an' rest a bit."

He made himself comfortable. "As I was saying, your Healer sounds like a very interesting woman. I believe she and I could benefit if we had a chance to get together and talk."

Alma Lee smiled. "I'll shore tell her that ya wants ta talk with her. Maybe ya can come visit up the holler. Granny is the most carin' an' lovin' woman I know. I believe she'll gladly share some of her secrets with ya. She'd git a big kick outta how funny ya talk, too." She pulled the sheet up over her mouth and giggled.

He couldn't help but chuckle at her last statement. "I promise I'll work on how I speak before I visit you in the hollow."

"Before I go, I need to check your incision to make sure it is healing properly." He gently lifted the bandage. "You're healing nicely. I believe we can let you go home tomorrow."

Alma Lee sat up straight. "That shore do sound fine ta me." She reached out and shook his hand. "I really want ta thank ya, Doctor, an' don't ya worry none 'bout me fergit'n ta tell Granny."

He smiled as he walked out of the room. *Learn how to talk correctly, isn't that a hoot!*

The following day, Alma Lee stood at the window, absent-mindedly twisting a strand of her long, red hair as she watched the morning traffic below. Her only thoughts were of Winder Hollow and when she would be home where she felt safe.

Her thoughts wandered to Jacob. *I wonder how Jacob is gittin' along at Mamie's place. I pray he's ok.* Her musing was interrupted by Dr. Lane's sudden appearance.

Alma Lee saw the look on his face and knew something good was about to happen. A big smile spread across his face. "Young lady, you get to go home this morning. So, let's get the bandage on your incision changed and then you can get dressed. I have already written the release order."

In her excitement, Alma Lee reached over and shook Mamie by the shoulder. "Mamie, wake up! Dr. Lane says I can go home."

Mamie sat up and rubbed the sleep from her eyes. Alma Lee walked over and gave Dr. Lane a big hug. She began to cry as a sense of relief washed over her. "Doctor, I want ta thank ya fer all ya has done fer me. I shore do hope ya come visit us back in Winder Holler. I promise ta tell Granny Harris ya wants ta meet her."

He hugged her gently in return. "It'll be my pleasure to come visit one of these days. I'm sure Miz Mamie will provide me with a phone number that I can call ahead of time and set up my visit. While I'm visiting, I'll come and see how you are feeling. Would that be okay with the two of you?"

Both Mamie and Alma Lee nodded their approval. Mamie spoke up. "I don't rightly have a telephone at my house, but the number I give you will get the message to me. You just tell them when you plan on visitin', and I'll see that Granny gets the message. She will be waitin' on you, along with a ride to the holler. You had best get an early start though, 'cause it's a far piece from Cove Mountain to the holler where Granny lives. It's goin' to take you all day to get there and back."

He gave each of them a big hug. "I'll be calling real soon. I wouldn't miss this trip for the world." With a spring in his step he walked down the hallway. His smile broadened as his spirit soared with the prospect of visiting Winder Hollow.

When the doctor left, Mamie's face broke into a wide grin. She chuckled. "Alma Lee, honey, I do believe the good doctor is sweet on you."

Alma Lee blushed at Mamie's remark. She turned her back to Mamie, removed her hospital gown and began to get dressed for the trip home. "Mamie, I think Dr. Lane is a right nice man, but he most likely treats all of his patients with kindness. Don't ya think?"

Mamie slapped her leg, tilted her head back and let out a loud cackling laugh, "Girl, you surely do have a lot to learn 'bout men."

Just then, the door opened and a male orderly walked in pushing a wheelchair.

Alma Lee took one look at it. "What in tarnation is that contraption?"

The orderly rocked his large frame back on his heels and put a hand to his chest. In mock indignation he said, "Contraption! No, young lady, this is my finest set of wheels. It's the wheelchair that brought you into the hospital and it's the wheelchair that is taking you out. Hospital rules, so climb in and let's get going. You are really going to enjoy the ride down in the elevator, too."

Alma Lee gave him a skeptical look, but did as she was told. All the way down the hall she wondered, *What in the world could an elevator be?* Before she knew it, the doors to the elevator opened with a *"Whoosh."* She was wheeled in. The orderly pushed the down button and the elevator dropped with a lurch.

Alma Lee gripped the arms of the wheelchair and let out a shaky, "Who-o-o-a! That shore did make my stomach feel strange."

When they reached the main floor, he wheeled her over to the front door, where Mamie was waiting with the car idling. He opened the car door and helped her slide into the front seat. Just as he was shutting the door, Alma Lee looked up at him with a big grin. "I shore would like ta go fer a ride in that there elevator one more time. It were lots of fun. Thanks fer the ride in your contraption, too."

The orderly saluted smartly. "It was my pleasure Ma'am." He laughed, spun the wheelchair around and waved over his shoulder as the hospital doors closed behind him.

Mamie put the car in gear and headed for the road that would take them back to Cove Mountain. Once they reached the city limits, Mamie reached over and patted Alma Lee's hand. "Don't you be worryin' none child. I will be drivin' a whole lot slower on the way home, so you just set back and enjoy the ride."

Alma Lee gave her a carefree smile. "An' don't ya be worryin' none either, Mamie, 'cause I promise I won't be screamin' the way I did when ya was bringin' me ta the hospital."

Those were just the words Mamie was hoping to hear. She settled herself comfortably into the well-worn seat and began to hum softly. She was looking forward to getting back to her home and way of life in Cove Mountain.

Chapter 13

Jacob and Hillard sat on Mamie's front porch. They looked out at the far away mountains. The rain had finally let up. The low-lying clouds and fog had lifted from the valley floor shortly after breakfast. They breathed in the crisp morning air, and the warm sun felt good upon their faces.

The fall season was at its peak. The mountain slopes were covered with a rich blanket of vivid colors, as the maple and poplar trees had turned shades of red, orange and yellow. The serenity they felt as they gazed upon the mountains made them homesick for the hollow.

Hillard sat facing the mountains and whittled on a piece of wood as he whistled a tune. Jacob broke his melancholy trance, looked over at Hillard. "What ya whittlin'?"

Hillard stopped his whistling and brushed the wood shavings off his lap. "Nothin', I'm just killin' time. It's a comfort ta me."

Jacob smiled. "Hain't that view somethin' else, Hillard. I shore do love this time of the year. I believe we is goin' ta have an early winter the way the leaves is turnin' so quick. Don't ya think, Hillard?"

Hillard glanced at the mountains. "Yep." He turned the piece of wood in his hand, found just the right spot and resumed his whittling.

"Did ya see that big old garden of Mamie's out back, Hillard?" Jacob asked. "She shore does plant lots of stuff." He let his eyes roam about the spacious porch, and added, "I don't believe she could get any more buckets of flowers settin' on this here porch railin', either. They shore are pretty." Jacob looked out across the wide valley. "I truly wish Alma Lee were here ta enjoy all of this."

The words no sooner left his mouth than Mamie's car rounded the corner and skidded to a stop in the driveway. In one easy motion, Jacob jumped out of his chair, leaped the porch railing and raced to the car. His face lit up as he saw Alma Lee. Jacob pulled open the car door and gently helped her from the car. He held her at arm's length, and in a rush of words, said, "Alma Lee, ya shore do look fine."

The two let out a joyful holler. They embraced each other as tears of joy streamed down their cheeks. They both tried to talk at the same time. Jacob reached out and cradled his sister's chin in his hand, tipping her face up to his. "I missed ya so much these past few days, an' I was worried 'bout ya."

Alma Lee leaned her head against his shoulder and whispered, "I missed ya a whole bunch, too. It shore is good ta be back with ya." She wrapped her arms around his waist and gave him a big sisterly hug.

Jacob took her by the arm and led her to the porch. He helped her into one of the comfortable, wooden chairs with the brightly colored cushions on them. He sat next to her and stared in disbelief that they were together again. He had many questions to ask her, but hardly knew where to begin.

Mamie, in her deep gravely voice, broke the spell. "Would you look at the two of you? A person would think you'd been apart for a year or more." She stepped up onto the porch and looked each of them in the eye, and added, "I don't know about the three of you, but I've had enough hospital food to last me a lifetime. Let's get in the house and I'll cook us all a proper meal." She didn't have to coax them. They were all eager for a good, home-cooked meal and a chance to sit back, relax and get caught up on what had happened while they were apart.

On the way into the house, Hillard bent down, hugged Alma Lee and planted a soft kiss on her cheek. He mumbled, "Shore am glad ya got all better." He held the door for Alma Lee to enter, and then ducked his head as he walked into the house.

After a good night's sleep and a hearty breakfast, it was time to make the long trip to Winder Hollow. Hillard had gone to fetch his wagon and team of mules from the neighbor's barn, while Alma Lee and Jacob said their goodbyes to Mamie.

Mamie stepped off of the porch and joined Jacob and Alma Lee in the front yard. She handed Jacob a large sack. "I know the three of you have got a right long ride ahead, so I packed the rest of the fried chicken we had yesterday and three big pieces of cornbread." She turned her head and looked Jacob in the eyes. "I trust you will save some of these vittles for old Hillard." Mamie chuckled. "Alma Lee, that brother of yours would eat the whole sack full if you didn't watch him close."

Jacob blushed. He leaned down, put his arm around her shoulder and kissed her cheek. Jacob opened the sack and breathed deeply of the aroma that greeted him. "Miz Mamie, I shore do like y'ur fried chicken. Now, if I can only git Alma Lee ta learn how ta cook it right. . ." The words had no sooner passed his lips when Alma Lee punched him in the shoulder.

"Jacob, I do believe your sister is feeling much better," Mamie said.

The sound of laughter was still heavy in the air when they heard the plodding of the mules' hooves on the gravel road. They looked up as Hillard rounded the corner to Mamie's house. At the driveway, he brought the wagon to a stop. Hillard tilted his head back, spit a stream of tobacco juice over the side of the wagon and peered out at them from under his hat. Jacob and Alma Lee knew it was time to go.

Alma Lee turned to Mamie, wrapped her arms around Mamie, choking back tears. "Mamie, I shore do appreciate everythin' ya has done fer me. If it's alright with ya, I would like ta come visit ya someday."

Mamie patted her gently on the back and then held her out at arms-length. "Child, you are welcome to visit anytime you want. I figure it's 'bout time you got out of the holler now and then."

She turned to Jacob. "I 'spect you should come along, too. Maybe Hillard can use some help when he comes to pick up supplies for the little store in the holler." Mamie walked Alma Lee over to the wagon. "Now, you best get in the wagon and head on up the trail. You tell Granny I will come visit one of these days. Don't forget to tell her 'bout the visit from Dr. Lane."

The wagon creaked as Jacob lifted his sister up onto the footboard of the wagon. Hillard offered her a calloused hand as she slid in next to him. Jacob gave Mamie one last peck on the cheek and clamored aboard.

With everyone on board, Hillard slapped the reins to the back of the mules. He raised his arm high into the air and gave a single wave without looking back, as was his custom. Alma Lee and Jacob took one last look at their new friend, gave one final wave and settled in for the long journey back to Winder Hollow.

Mamie shaded her eyes against the morning sun. The wagon kicked up dust as it turned the corner and disappeared from sight. She felt sad at their leaving and with a heavy heart, she turned and walked slowly toward the house.

Chapter 14

For the first three miles of the trip, Hillard, Alma Lee and Jacob chattered non-stop. Alma Lee hardly took a breath as she recounted to Jacob and Hillard all the things she had seen at the hospital in Fairmont.

It wasn't long before the steady cadence of the mules' hooves lulled each of them into their own thoughts and conversation died out. Memories of her stay at the hospital vanished as Alma Lee gazed reflectively out across the wide valley before her. She spotted a lone hawk riding the rising thermals as it soared higher and higher into the cloudless sky. It floated effortlessly in quiet solitude. A wave of contentment washed over Alma Lee as the anxiety she had endured released its cruel grip.

"I shore don't know 'bout the two of ya, but this shore is a right pretty trip back ta the holler. I don't rightly remember any of this when we left the holler."

With a smirk, Hillard glanced at Jacob. Jacob snickered, poked him in the ribs, and they burst out laughing.

"What the two of ya laughin' 'bout?"

Jacob took time to catch his breath before he spoke. "Alma Lee, ya was so durn drunk from the hard licker Granny give ya, that ya was doin' nothin' but sleepin' an' snorin' right hard back there in the bottom of the wagon." Jacob and Hillard began to laugh again. Tears streamed down their cheeks.

It was mid-day when they reached the river they had to ford before entering the hollow. Thankfully, the rain had stopped a couple of days earlier and the river was back to its normal level. As Hillard eased the mules down the bank, he smiled at Jacob, "Well, at least this time I won't have ta be takin' me a cold bath." He chuckled and urged the mules on.

Several miles further, they entered the wide mouth of the hollow. It was a dry, sunny, fall day. As they traveled deeper into the hollow, everyday sounds and smells assured them all was well.

The heavy scent of wood smoke, floating lazily on the breeze, aroused a rush of pleasant memories in each of them. The distant buzzing of a chainsaw signaled that someone was laying in their winter firewood.

Alma Lee broke their silence. "It shore is good to be back in the holler an' hear the wind blowing through the tree tops an' be able to hear the birds singin'. I sure don't miss the sounds of the big city."

As the wagon broke over the next rise, Granny's cabin came into view. They were about to pass by, when Granny stepped out on her porch and hollered out. "Would ya look at the three of ya? I shore am glad ya finally got back. Ya git down from that wagon an' come set a spell. I want ta hear all 'bout y'ur trip. Jacob, ya help Alma Lee down. I don't want her tearin' any of them stitches out."

Granny reached her hand out, helped Alma Lee up onto the porch and ushered her over to a large rocking chair. "Ya best sit in this here rocker of mine. It's the most comfortable one I has an' it'll treat ya right."

Alma Lee eased herself into the rocker.

Granny turned to Hillard. "Hillard, would ya go inside an' fetch three of them kitchen chairs fer the rest of us."

Hillard returned with the chairs? Granny chose the one next to Alma Lee. She steadied herself on the arm of the rocker, and with a helping hand from Alma Lee, lowered herself into the chair. As she pushed her spectacles back in place, she reached over to Alma Lee and took her hand in hers. "Child, ya shore look a whole lot better than ya did a few days back. How are ya feelin' since the doctor took out y'ur appendix?"

Alma Lee smiled. "Granny, I shore do want ta thank ya fer sendin' me outta the holler ta that there hospital. Dr. Lane, that's the doctor who operated on me, is a right nice man. He fixed me up just fine. He said it was a good thing ya knowed what my trouble was, 'cause I was in a bad way. He said he'd like to come one day to visit an' share some healin' things with ya. I told him ya would probably like ta do just that." Then with a devilish laugh she added, "Ya have ta listen real close like when he talks, 'cause he talks kinda funny. Mamie said he jest has a different accent, is all."

Granny slapped both of her hands on her knees and let out a laugh that shook her whole body. The tears trickled down her cheeks. Between fits of laughter she managed to say, "Child, I reckon ya found out a whole bunch 'bout life outta the holler. Some of it must have been right frightful fer ya, but findin' out first hand 'bout folks outta the holler talkin' different is right hilarious."

Granny wiped away the tears with a corner of her apron. "Darlin, I do believe the good doctor jest might have had a little problem understandin' the way ya talk, too."

Alma Lee pursed her lips and contemplated what Granny had said. After a moment or two of silence she threw up her arms. "Why in the world would a body have trouble understandin' how I talk? I don't talk any different than the rest of ya, an' ya'll sound right fine ta me."

Jacob and Hillard burst out laughing. "Alma Lee, Jacob managed to say, I do believe ya needs ta git out of this holler a bit more. An' ya jest might find y'urself a husband who'll take ya away from all of this. That is, if he can understand ya." He doubled over with laughter, holding his sides.

Doubled over like he was, Jacob didn't even see it coming. Just as he straightened up, Alma Lee gave him a backhand to his chest, so quick and hard, it almost knocked him off his chair.

Hillard let out a sympathetic, "Oh-h-h-h!" "Jacob, I do believe y'ur sister is feelin' a whole heap better. If I was ya, I wouldn't be settin' or standin' close ta her when ya open y'ur mouth so."

Jacob was shocked. Finally he managed to catch his breath. "I do believe we best git her home right quick, afore she gits much better. I don't believe my poor body could stand another blow like that one."

Granny planted her hands firmly on her hips. "If the three of ya are done havin' so much fun, maybe it's 'bout time fer y'all to climb back aboard the wagon. Ya will find we stocked up y'ur place with wood fer heatin' an' cookin'. All y'ur neighbors an' kin folks put in a supply of food fer ya. I'll be checkin' in on ya in a couple of days an' see how ya are gettin' along. I 'spect the doctor will be wantin' ta see how ya is doin', too. I'll be comin' with him when he visits."

Granny placed one hand on her knee and the other on the back of Alma Lee's chair and steadied herself as she stood on shaky legs. She let out a slight wheeze as she struggled to stand erect. Once she had her legs under her, she looked to Alma Lee. "Did the good doctor say when he might git ta come visit?"

Alma Lee stood and put her arm around Granny's shoulder. "He didn't rightly say, Granny, but I'm lookin' forward ta his visit. He's a right nice feller an' shore has a friendly way 'bout him. Mamie says he's sweet on me. I told her I didn't believe it, but the more I think on it, he just might be."

Jacob snickered. "Alma Lee, I do believe you've done more than think on it, by the way ya talked 'bout him most of the way home. Dr. Lane this an' Dr. Lane that. Hain't that right, Hillard?"

Hillard eased himself out of the chair, plopped his hat on his head and smiled wide. "Yep, she shore did."

Alma Lee blushed.

The mules quickened their pace after leaving Granny's cabin. They knew their barn was only a short distance up the hollow. The trip had been hard on them and they needed a rest.

The three weary travelers were lost in their own thoughts, as the familiar sights and sounds of the hollow rolled by.

A warm breeze floated down the hollow, lifting brightly colored leaves from the ground, scattering them about. The mid-day sun was hot. The dank earthy smell of the forest, along with the decaying fall leaves sent a heady aroma floating on the breeze. It brought back memories of their youth and the promise of pleasant days ahead.

The mules steady plodding lulled Jacob and Alma Lee into a sleepy state. Just as the wagon jolted over a rut in the road, Hillard nudged Alma Lee and pointed. There in the distance stood their log cabin. As they drew closer to the cabin, tears of joy slide down Alma Lee's cheeks. She reached over, put her arms around her brother and laid her head on his shoulder. In a soft voice, she whispered, "Jacob, we is finally home."

In his own way, Hillard understood the emotions she was feeling. He placed his hand gently on her head and in a gesture of understanding, ruffled her long, red hair and smiled down at her.

Hillard pulled the wagon up along side the path to the cabin. Jacob jumped down and extended a strong, muscular arm to Alma Lee.

Hillard reached under the seat, pulled out the feed sacks containing their spare clothing and passed them down to Jacob.

Jacob set the sacks down, reached up and shook their friend's hand. "Hillard, we shore do thank ya fer everythin' ya done fer us. I promise I'll make it up ta ya, someway."

Hillard looked down at them with a sheepish grin, "It twern't nothin'," he said slowly, "an' ya don't owe me nary a thing. Jest remember, we is holler folks, an' we take care of our own." With that he smiled, slapped the reins to the mules, turned the wagon around and headed back down the hollow.

Jacob picked up the sacks of clothing and the two of them walked up the path to the cabin.

Their eyes swept from one corner of the cabin to the other. They couldn't believe what their neighbors and kinfolks had done for them. Just as Granny had said, the wood bins were full and the pantry was stocked with all kinds of home-canned goods. They found a note on the freshly-scrubbed kitchen table telling them there was a fresh cured ham in the smokehouse.

The inside of the cabin had been swept clean, scrubbed down, and all of the windows sparkled. It was obvious that the place had been left to air out from the stench of sickness. To top it all off, both of the mattresses on their beds had been replaced.

They stood in the middle of the cabin arm-in-arm, and looked around in amazement. Silently they gave thanks for all that had been done for them and for being home in Winder Hollow.

Chapter 15

Three weeks later

"Hello, Dobbs' store."

"Yes Ma'am. This is Dr. Lane from Fairmont. Miz Mamie Cogar gave me this number and said I could get a message to her."

"Yes, Doctor. You just tell me what you want to say, and I'll see she gets the message."

"Tell her that I can drive to Cove Mountain first thing Friday morning. Also, I have borrowed a 4-wheel drive truck to help get to Winder Hollow. Would you also tell her that I hope she can go with me? If she has any questions she can give me a call."

"I'll see she gets the message, Doctor. You have a good day now."

"Thank you, Ma'am, I appreciate your help."

He had no sooner hung up, when he felt a shiver of excitement. He felt a gentle tug at the corners of his mouth, as his smile widened with the prospect of making the long anticipated journey to Winder Hollow.

His mind raced with thoughts of meeting Granny Harris, the hollow Healer. And the prospect of seeing Alma Lee once again and experiencing the life she talked so much about. Just the thought, gave him a giddy feeling, like a boy going out on his first date.

Daylight had not yet returned to the mountains as Dr. Lane placed a small backpack on the passenger seat of the truck. He fired up the engine and turned on the windshield wiper to clear away the heavy morning dew. Once the motor had warmed, he clicked on the heater, turned the radio on and headed out toward the city limits and the distant town of Cove Mountain.

For the most part, the city of Fairmont had not yet awakened from its nightly slumber, and the drive out of town was unusually quiet. Within minutes, he had reached the turn that would take him over the mountains to his destination. The prospect of the day that loomed before him brought a smile to his face. He relaxed his grip on the wheel and let the soothing music transport him to another place, leaving the rigors of city life behind.

The speeding truck sailed around a sweeping curve and the small hamlet of Cove Mountain could be seen in the wide valley below. His pulse quickened at the sight before him as the sky blazed pink from the approaching sunrise. He watched intently as the streetlights below blinked off one at a time in response to the descending early morning light. As the road transported him closer and closer to his destination the twists and turns of the steep mountain road lulled him into a state of well-being.

Once he had reached the valley floor, it was only a short drive to the center of town. He pulled over and took the directions to Mamie's house from his pack. He was relieved to find he was only a few blocks away. Just past the post office, he made a right. He drove the deserted street at a slow speed, not wanting to miss her house.

Two blocks later, he spotted her on the front porch watering the many potted plants that filled the porch railing. She looked up and waved as he pulled into her drive. "Howdy, Dr. Lane, I see you had no trouble findin' the place."

He stepped from the truck and joined her on the porch. Mamie set the watering can down and gave him a warm welcoming hug. "It shore is good to see you again, Doctor."

He smiled down at her. "It's good to see you too, Miz Mamie. I see you're doing well."

She gave him a flip of her hand and said, "I'm doin' right fine, but you can just call me Mamie, everyone does."

He chuckled. "Well then, Mamie, you just call me Robert. I would like that a lot."

"Well then, Robert, I 'spect you are anxious to get to Winder Holler and meet Granny." She turned to go into the house, stopped mid-stride and said, "I do believe you mentioned that you wanted to check on Alma Lee, too. Didn't you?" Before he could answer, she turned her head and gave him one of her sly winks and laughed. The look on his face was the only answer she needed. She laughed again. "That's what I thought."

Robert blushed at her candor. As he groped for an appropriate reply, he sniffed the air. "Mamie, is that fresh coffee I smell?"

She stopped at the threshold and held the screen door open for him. "You come right on in. I've got half a pot of coffee left and it's still hot. Grab a couple of mugs out of the cupboard there by the stove. We can take em with us. Let me grab my hat and jacket and we can be on our way.

Robert retrieved the mugs and filled them full. He took a sip. "This coffee sure tastes good, Mamie, It's a whole bunch better than the cup of instant I had back at my apartment."

Mamie walked into the kitchen with her hat on and her jacket over her arm. "I tried that instant coffee once, but didn't cotton much to the taste." She took the mug of coffee he offered, took a big swallow and smacked her lips. "Now, that's what I call a good cup of coffee." She gave him a satisfied smile.

Robert held the screen door open for her as she took one last look around the kitchen, turned off the light and closed the door behind her. Robert offered her his arm.

When they reached the truck, he pushed his pack out of the way and helped Mamie into the passenger's seat.

Once inside, he buckled up and helped Mamie with her seatbelt. He smiled at her. "There, that should keep you nice and safe."

Mamie looked at him, raised an eyebrow and said, "I thank you for the help, but how fast do you think your goin' to be drivin'?"

He gave her a perplexed look. "I thought we were going to drive part way to the hollow?"

"We are," she said, "but that old road, if that's what you want to call it, isn't much more than a wagon trail. Don't you be worrin' none, Robert, 'cause we have got plenty of time to get where we are goin'.

Hillard is goin' to meet us at the river. We have to cross it to get to the holler. We have plenty of time to drive nice and safe."

Mamie reached over and gave him a reassuring pat on the knee. "I know you're really excited to meet Granny and all, so let's get goin'."

Robert put the truck in gear and backed out of the driveway. "Which way do we go, Mamie?"

She pointed up the road. "Go on up to the corner, Robert, and turn left. That will get us headin' toward Winder Holler."

Those were the words he had wanted to hear. He felt a flutter in the pit of his stomach as a smile spread across his face. The day was ripe for adventure and held great promise. He would never remember making that first left turn.

Chapter 16

The ride to the river and their rendezvous with Hillard was as Mamie predicted.

The road was heavily damaged by the ravages of the recent storms. Potholes and deep ruts made driving tedious.

Mamie sat on the edge of the seat to scout the road ahead. "You're doin' just fine, Robert." She braced herself as the truck dropped into another deep rut.

Robert jerked hard on the wheel and the truck responded as all four wheels sprayed clumps of mud in their wake.

Robert let out a loud, "Phew!" as he struggled to calm his shattered nerves. He wiped his sweaty palms. Breathlessly, he asked, "Is it much further to the river, Mamie?"

Mamie chuckled. "It's not more than a mile ahead. The road levels off some and should be a might easier goin'." She released her white-knuckled grip on the dash, scooted back on the seat and patted him reassuringly on the shoulder.

Robert relaxed his clenched jaw. "That sounds good to me, Mamie. My poor arms are getting tired from jerking on the wheel." He smiled tentatively and willed his hands to stop shaking. To calm his nerves, he hummed to himself and blocked out all thoughts, but what lay ahead at the end of the road.

The truck descended down a slight downgrade and passed through a pocket of cool morning air, heavy with the mixed scent of wildflowers and dried meadow grasses. Mamie breathed deeply as the cab filled with the subtle smells that swirled around her. "I sure do miss making this trip back to the holler." She looked out across the open fields and heavily forested slopes and sighed. "I spect it's goin' on two years since I last visited my cousin. Lord, I do miss livin' back in the mountains."

Out of the corner of his eye, Robert spotted the faraway look on her wrinkled face. Her misty hazel eyes shimmered in the morning light. She sniffed and wiped her nose on her shirt-sleeve.

Robert was jolted back into the task of steering the truck, when Mamie shook his shoulder and stabbed her finger toward a distant spot. "Look there, Robert! I see Hillard and his mules waitin' for us at the river. Do you see him, Robert?" She stuck her head out the window, waved and shouted, "Hey, Hillard!" Not getting any response, she reached over and laid on the horn. Hillard's head jerked up. He stood slowly to his full height and waved his old hat wildly above his head. Mamie slapped her leg and let out a loud "Whoop!" "That Hillard can take a nap at the drop of a hat," she cackled.

Robert leaned forward to get a better look as the truck closed the gap between them and Hillard. He sucked in a deep breath. "Would you look at the size of that man?"

Mamie snickered. "Shoot, Robert, he's nothing but a big old boy. He's got a heart of gold, a smile for everyone he meets, and he's as gentle as a kitten. One couldn't ask for a better friend than Hillard."

The truck jolted over a deep rut and came to a stop next to the wagon. Robert turned to Mamie. "Hold on, Mamie, and I'll help you down. . ." He was too late. She was already half-way out of the truck. He shook his head and smiled as she made her way toward the wagon with outstretched arms to greet her friend.

Robert had no sooner exited the truck, when Hillard, in one easy motion, jumped from the wagon and landed with a resounding thud. He felt the ground quiver around him as the huge man scooped Mamie up with one arm, wiped his hand on his overalls and extended it toward him. "Ya must be Dr. Lane. I've heard a whole heap 'bout ya from Alma Lee. Granny says she can hardly wait ta meet ya, too."

Robert's smile broadened at the mention of Alma Lee. He took the hand that was offered and watched with apprehension as it disappeared into Hillard's grip. He let out a sigh of relief and managed a weak smile at Hillard's firm but gentle handshake. "It is a pleasure to meet you, Hillard," he said, as he retrieved his hand and flexed his fingers. "I understand that you were the one who brought Alma Lee out of the hollow. If it hadn't been for your efforts, she might not have survived."

Hillard stared at the ground. "It twern't nothin' at all, Doctor. Us holler folks do what has ta be done ta help one another. That's jest how it's done back in these here mountains."

Robert reached up and placed his hand on Hillard's broad shoulder. "Maybe so, but it was a remarkable thing you did."

Mamie wriggled out of Hillard's grip, patted his ample belly and hugged him tight. "He's right, Hillard. Alma Lee is here today because of you and the good doctor. Now, we best get goin' to the holler. Time's a wastin' and I 'spect Granny is waitin' on us."

Hillard looked down at her. "Yep. There was light shining from Granny's cabin and she had her cook stove fired up. I could see smoke trailin' from the chimney as I went by." In one easy motion, he reached down and scooped Mamie up in his arms, placed her on the wagon seat and climbed in beside her.

Robert headed to the other side of the wagon. As he passed close to one of the mules, he ran his hand over its back and patted it lightly. The sweet smell of hay greeted him as he approached the front of the mule. "These sure are some fine looking mules, Hillard. I've never been this close to one." The words had no sooner passed his lips, when the closest mule raised its head and let out an ear-shattering bray. Robert jumped back as if he had been bitten. As the last of the sound echoed off the near mountain side, Robert looked up at Hillard and Mamie. His face was pale, his eyes wide and his hand was pressed tight against his chest. He sucked in a deep breath and felt his legs go weak. "Lord, I wasn't expecting that," he said breathlessly. With shaky hands, he extended his arm to the mule in an attempt to steady himself. Hesitantly he patted the mule on the neck and mustered a wry smile. The mule, in turn, nuzzled him, seeking more attention.

From high on the wagon came a chorus of laughter as Hillard and Mamie watched the scene play out before them. Hillard could hardly contain himself and was bent over in a fit of laughter. "Doc, I do believe my mule has taken a shine ta ya."

Robert, feeling the color rise in his cheeks, took several steps forward, when Mamie piped up and stopped him in his tracks. "Hold on there, Robert, I do believe you left your poke in the truck."

He gave her a quizzical look. "My what?"

"That cloth bag with straps on it, you left it in the truck."

Robert shook his head and turned to retrace his steps to the truck. He looked both mules in the eyes and said, "I'll be right back." With the backpack retrieved and slung over his shoulder, he climbed aboard the wagon.

Hillard removed the reins from around the brake handle and was about to slap them to the back of the mules, when Robert stopped him. "Hold on, Hillard, I forgot to lock the truck."

Hillard grinned and urged the mules forward. "Don't ya be worrin', Doc. There hain't a soul 'round who'll bother it. We don't have locks on our doors back in the holler, either."

Mamie patted him on the leg. "It'll be alright, Robert. Don't you fret none. You're among mountain folks, now."

Robert leaned back on the seat, his head held low. "I'm sorry about that, Hillard. I guess I've got a lot to learn."

Hillard gave him a sideways glance. "Yep," he said as he spit a stream of tobacco juice over the side and wiped his lips with the back of his hand.

Robert griped the side of the seat, as the mules pulled the wagon down the steep embankment. He watched them strain against their harness, as the strong current fought their progress across the cool, dark waters of the river.

The steady plodding of the mules hooves and the beauty of the ever-changing scenery lulled Robert into a state of quiet content. He listened as Mamie wove a thread of stories, nonstop, about her life as a young girl growing up in the holler. Robert bolted upright, as she abruptly hollered out, "Look there, Robert!" She pointed to a spot between the two mountain sides that towered over them. "See the gap in the tree line over there. That's the entrance to Winder Holler."

Robert shaded his eyes. "I see it, Mamie. I've waited what seems like an eternity to see the hollow. My interest was peaked by the stories Alma Lee shared with me about her life there. I hope she remembers our conversations and my promise that I would come visit her."

Mamie chuckled. "Oh, I wouldn't worry 'bout her forgettin', Robert. I 'spect she's been sittin' on pins and needles ever since I got the message to Granny that you was comin' to visit today. News travels fast in the holler. You just wait and see."

The dense forest of the hollow wrapped slowly around them as the constant creak of the wagon wheels kept cadence to the plodding of the mules' hooves. Sunlight filtered through the canopy, casting a kaleidoscope of ever changing shadows and light patterns upon the forest floor.

Mamie watched out of the corner of her eye, as Robert's eyes darted from left to right and back again as he tried to soak in the beauty that surrounded them. "What do you think so far, Robert?" she asked.

"This is truly amazing, Mamie. I haven't had the opportunity to explore much outside of the city since I moved here. The trip across the mountains and to the river was great, but this is so beautiful. I've never felt so at peace in my entire life."

Mamie placed her hand lightly on his and smiled. "I know just how you feel, Robert," she whispered, "I get a little maudlin myself every time I make the trip back. I miss the smell of the forest, its cool presence and all the critters that make this place their home. I truly do."

Robert stole a glance in Hillard's direction. His drooped head and a slight snoring affirmed that Hillard was fast asleep. Robert nudged Mamie with his elbow and nodded his head in Hillard's direction.

Mamie snickered. "I told you he could sleep at the drop of a hat." Robert's wrinkled brow drew her attention, as he stared at Hillard. "Don't you worry, Robert. These old mules know every twist and turn in the road. They'll stop on their own if there's a problem."

With each passing minute, the steady pace of the mules brought them deeper into the hollow. Mamie and Robert looked to one another, as the natural sounds of the forest gave way to the steady rhythm of someone chopping wood, mixed with the excited laughter of children playing. A short while later, just as the wagon cleared a maze of heavy underbrush a log cabin came into view. At the sight of the wagon, the man set his axe against the chopping block and mopped his sweaty brow with his shirt sleeve. The wagon and driver he knew well. He waved and shouted, "Hey there, Hillard."

Hillard's head jerked up with a start. Mamie and Robert were staring at him, trying their best to contain there amusement. To ease Hillard's confusion, Mamie pointed to the man who had shouted. "He's over there, Hillard."

Hillard swung his head in the direction where Mamie pointed. Spotting the man who had called out, he hollered back, "Hey there y'urself." Then he wiped the drool from the corner of his mouth and grinned sheepishly at having been caught napping.

Mamie chuckled, waved to the man, and playfully poked Hillard in the ribs. Hillard's face turned bright red, as she knew it would.

Robert sat quietly, lost in thought, as they passed cabin after cabin along the winding road. The sound of the small creek next to the road held him spellbound as it tumbled over jumbled rocks and coursed its way through the hollow.

A cabin set back in an open glade came into view as they cleared an outcropping of rocks. There, on the side porch of the cabin, was an old woman scrubbing clothes in a metal tub. A clothesline strung between two trees was half full of clean clothes flapping in the breeze. The sound of the mules' hooves caught her attention. She looked up, tucked an errant strand of hair behind her ear, and hollered out as she recognized the driver. "Mornin', Hillard." She took a second look and squinted. "Mamie, is that you? Lord, I haven't seen you in a coon's age."

Mamie waved her hand wildly. "It's me for sure. I'll stop on the way back and howdy you proper. Right now, we have got to get Dr. Lane to Granny's place."

The woman looked at Robert. "Nice to see you Doctor. I heard ya was comin' ta visit. Granny's plumb excited 'bout meetin' ya."

Robert smiled and waved at the woman.

Mamie leaned close. "What'd I tell you, Robert? News travels fast in the holler."

Robert grinned and shook his head. "Yes, you did, Mamie. Yes, you did."

As the wagon topped a rise in the road, a veil of smoke covered the lowland before them. The tops of small trees and bushes were the only things that could be seen poking through the dense smoke. The morning chill held it captive, close to the ground.

The wagon descended the slope and Robert tentatively sniffed the cool air. "I don't know what's causing the smoke, but it sure smells nice and sweet."

Hillard pointed off to the right. "If ya look way back in them trees, ya can see the roof of a cabin and the smokehouse out back."

Robert stood and craned his neck to see where Hillard had pointed. "Ah, yes. I can see them now. What are they doing?"

Hillard pulled the mules to a stop. "They is smokin' the hams an' side meat from the hogs they butchered a couple of days ago."

Robert, jolted by the sudden stop, sat down. "What makes the smoke smell so good?"

Hillard removed his hat and scratched his head. "By the smell of it, he's usin' hickory and sassafras wood fer the smoke. The extra sweetness ya smell is the sugar cure rub he put on the meat."

"You can tell all of that from just the smell?" Robert asked.

Mamie chuckled. "Shoot, Robert, Hillard knows all that stuff. He's a woodsman and was born right here in the holler." She gave Hillard a nudge. "Go ahead, Hillard, tell him 'bout yourself."

Hillard removed the cud of tobacco from his cheek, tossed it over the side and began. "'Bout thirty-eight years ago, Granny helped Maw give birth ta me. I don't hardly remember much about that," he said, as he winked at Mamie. "But I've been told I weighed right close ta fifteen pounds when I was born."

Mamie chimed in. "Yep. You sure was a big one. I can remember the day as if it were yesterday. Granny knew it was goin' to be a tough birth, so she asked me to give her a hand. Thank the Lord she did. You were the biggest baby I ever laid eyes on." She put her hand on his shoulder and gave him a pat. "I recon that's why I hold him dear to my heart, he's the son I never had."

Mamie wiped the single tear that had collected in the corner of her eye, before it could slide down her cheek. "I'm sorry, Hillard, for interrupting you so. I just couldn't help myself. The memory of that day has always stayed with me."

Hillard draped his arm around her shoulder and gave it a gentle squeeze. Mamie nuzzled comfortably against him. "Go on now, Hillard, Robert is waitin' to here the rest."

Hillard prompted the mules forward and they headed into the smoke ladened flats below. He took a fresh chaw of tobacco and continued. "My paw was a woodsman and his paw before him. As far back as I can recollect, Paw was out cuttin' wood, sharpening his tools, or teaching me how ta use them proper. Maw always said I was born ta be a woodsman. She kept me and Paw well fed. Paw would always tease me by sayin', 'Ya know, Hillard, it'd be cheaper ta board ya out, than feed ya.' Maw laughed right hard every time he said that. Then she'd say, 'Now Paw, the boy is still growin', so ya let him eat.' And eat I did. I stopped growin' jest shy of six feet eight inches."

Robert sat quietly on the edge of the bench seat, fascinated by Hillard's life story. He gave a low whistle, as Hillard mentioned his height. "I knew you were tall, but I had no idea just how tall you are. And you are obviously very muscular. Do you mind me asking how much you weigh?"

Hillard chuckled. "Well, the last time I stepped on the scales at the feed supply store back in Cove Mountain, I was a shade over two hundred and ninety five pounds."

Mamie spoke up. "And nary a pound of fat to be found. Hillard's life of hard work has made him the strongest man in the holler. Did you see the size of this boy's hands, Robert? As she placed her hand next to Hillard's for emphasis.

Robert's thoughts reflected back to his handshake with Hillard. "I did indeed, Mamie. I was quite impressed with his firm grip."

Hillard's face flushed. He was eager to change the subject. With a slap of the reins, he encouraged the mules to quicken their pace. The shallow, smoke-filled valley was soon left behind and the wagon eased over the crest of the hill.

Hillard pointed to the sweeping curve ahead and the telltale curl of smoke that floated skyward. "Look over yonder. That's Granny's cabin, back off ta the left."

Robert and Mamie turned in unison toward the spot Hillard pointed to. Robert's pulse quickened as the cabin came into view and the prospect of finally meeting Granny was about to become a reality. His voice was tinged with excitement as he blurted out, "Mamie, I'm so excited to be meeting Granny. I feel just like a little boy on his first day of school."

Mamie held his hand and patted it gently. "Now, Robert, just relax. I know Granny is just as excited to meet the doctor who saved, Alma Lee. Just remember to take a deep breath when we get there, and don't forget your poke under the seat."

Mamie observed the nervous ball of energy seated next to her and couldn't help but think, *Lord! What is he going to be like when he gets to see, Alma Lee? Lordy!*

Chapter 17

Robert knew he had entered into a whole new realm of life, when he crossed the threshold of Granny's cabin. As his eyes grew accustomed to the dimly lit interior, the world of Granny Harris opened up to him. The soft glow emanating from the dying embers of the morning fire cast a warm and welcome feeling about the room. Bundles of drying herbs hung from wooden pegs alongside the fireplace. Their subtle aromas floated endlessly about the cabin. Along one log wall were pictures of children smiling back at him. He couldn't help but smile, as his eyes drifted from one happy face to another.

He felt a gentle touch on his shoulder. "Do ya like my wall of kids, Doctor?" Granny asked in a soft voice. She gave him a slight nudge. "Go on in. Ya can git a closer look if ya want."

As Robert walked hesitantly toward the pictures, the worn, wooden floor creaked beneath his feet. Mamie followed him over and stood motionless, as her eyes roamed the rows of pictures. She spotted the one she was looking for and touched it and proudly proclaimed, "This here one is, Hillard. He shore was a cute little boy."

Robert took a step closer. "Yes, he was, Mamie." Robert's brow wrinkled, as he reflected on his first meeting with Hillard that morning. "Now that I think about it, you can still see his boyish face and that great big smile of his."

Mamie laughed. "Yep, he shore does have a big smile. I told you he was nothin' but a big old boy." She laughed again and pointed out a few of the other children she knew personally.

Granny stood quietly next to her wood cook stove, watching the two of them. Their animated conversation brought a smile to her face. She retrieved her worn hot pad from the top of the warming oven and removed the pan of hot biscuits from the oven. Then she set three mugs on the scarred wooden table and removed the disc of wax from a jar of homemade wild strawberry jam. She set everything in place and waited for a lull in their conversation. "I 'spect the two of ya might be hungry after yer long trip here."

Robert's head jerked around at the mention of something to eat. "I thought I smelled something baking when I came in. Is that fresh perked coffee I smell, too?" The thought of something more than the bowl of cold cereal he had earlier that morning made his mouth water.

Mamie chimed in, "Come on, Robert, before she tosses it out to the hogs."

Robert chuckled. "Not on my watch, she won't. Those biscuits and coffee smell heavenly."

Robert hurried to the table, pulled out the chair for Granny and helped her into it. She looked up at him and smiled. "Lord, Mamie, I didn't know ya was bringin' me such a gentleman."

Robert bowed gracefully and helped Mamie into her chair. Mamie giggled as he slid the chair up to the table. "You best set down, Robert, before the coffee gets cold."

Granny clapped her hands together. "Amen. Now let's git ta eatin'." She passed the jar of jam to Robert, just as he helped himself to two warm biscuits. "Here, Dr. Lane, ya got ta try some of my strawberry jam. It goes right well with them hot biscuits."

Her eyes lit up with joy, as she watched him pile his biscuit high with the sweet jam and devoured half of it with one bite. Robert closed his eyes and let out a low groan, as the first mouth full caused his taste buds to explode. "Wow! That is good jam, Granny!" With a quick sip of the hot coffee, the second half followed the first. As he reached for the next biscuit, he caught Granny and Mamie both watching him, a big grin on each of their faces. He set his biscuit down. The color rose in his cheeks. "I'm sorry for acting like a starved man, but I've been a bachelor for way too long. Besides, I can't cook and this is a real treat for me."

Granny reached out and patted his hand. "You just take yer time Doctor..."

Mamie interrupted. "Granny, I do believe that you should know that Dr. Lane would prefer us to call him Robert. He says it makes him feel more at ease and like being back home with his kin."

Granny smacked her hand down on the table. "Then, Robert, it'll be. Now, Robert, ya eat all ya want an' when ya is finished, we'll talk 'bout healin'."

Robert took one last sip of coffee and retrieved his backpack he had stashed by the wall of pictures. He placed his spiral notebook and two pencils on the table. He took a wrapped package out of his pack and placed it in front of Granny. "This is a gift from me to you. I thought that you could possibly use it in your practice of healing back here in the hollow."

Granny's eyes opened wide as she hefted the weight of the package in her hands.

Mamie couldn't stand the suspense any longer. "Go on, Granny, open it. I've been thinkin' on what Robert had in that poke ever since I saw it."

Granny carefully peeled the tape away from the colorful wrapping paper, folded the paper neatly and set it aside for future use. Her eyes glistened as she ran her gnarled fingers lightly over the raised letters on the front of the thick book. She mumbled faintly, as she read each word embossed there, "Family Medical and Health Guide." She let her hand glide over the richly textured cover and then clutched it to her breast. "This is a right special gift, Robert. The one that was passed down ta me by my maw has seen better days. I don't rightly know how old it is, an' how outta date, but it has served me well. I thank ya much." She pulled him closer and kissed him on the cheek.

Robert smiled. "Is that how you knew what was wrong with Alma Lee and that she needed an operation to remove her appendix?"

"It sure was," she said proudly. "I have read that book so many times over the years, I can almost recite it from memory. But my memory is slippin' fast these days."

Robert watched as her smile faded, her shoulders slumped and the tired look of an old woman stared back at him. She gave him a half-hearted grin and continued. "I don't know if I has many more years left and the energy to be the Healer here in the holler. I'll be seventy-nine come spring time. My poor old body is startin' ta fail me, and my mule is 'bout all done in, too."

"Do you have someone in your family you could pass your knowledge of mountain healing onto?" Robert asked.

Granny shook her head. "I'm the last of my kin in the holler an' Mamie is the last one outside of the holler."

Mamie reached over and placed her hand on Granny's. "Don't ya worry none, Granny, we'll come up with something. The folks in the holler has got to have a Healer and a Healer they'll get."

With the mood growing more somber by the moment, Robert decided to change the subject. "Granny, are you up to sharing some of the natural ways of healing folks here in the hollow? I see many bundles of herbs hanging from the wall. Are those the ones you use in your poultices and medicines?"

"Yes they are, Robert. I has them dryin' by the fire afore I puts them away in sealed jars. I growed them herbs right here in my garden. I also gits some of the men ta pick me some of the wild plants I use, while they is out in the woods."

Robert opened his notepad and poised his pencil. "What kind of wild plants do you have them collect? And what do you use each of them for?"

Granny chuckled and eased herself from her chair and shuffled over to a large cabinet leaning against the wall. The old cabinet held an array of bottles of various sizes and colors crammed side by side on the sagging shelves. On top of the cabinet were piles of books stacked haphazardly. Granny pushed several books aside and plucked a thick folder bulging with old yellowed papers, from the pile. As she passed by her cook stove, she grabbed the coffee pot and poured each of them a fresh cup of coffee. Mamie took the pot from her hands, just as Granny laid the folder on the table and plopped into her chair. Granny pushed her spectacles up on her nose. "I'll do ya one better, Robert. She shoved the folder toward him and laid her hand on his arm. "This here is all of the remedies that I inherited from my maw, at the time of her death. And her maw used them before that. I 'spect everythin' in there is well over a hundred years old." She leaned back in her chair and took a sip from her mug. "What else ya want ta know?"

Robert opened the folder and began to leaf through the yellowed, curled pages. The handwritten pages were filled from top to bottom with a fine bold script. Many pages held small drawings of plants he had never seen and names unknown to him. He looked up at Granny and smiled. He continued to turn the pages slowly and methodically. He held them as if they were from some ancient, holy manuscript. He closed the folder and folded his hands before him. "Would it be possible for me to borrow this folder for a week? I would love to have a copy of it to study later."

Granny gave him a quizzical look, the wrinkles of her brow deepening. "I don't mind ya borrowin' it, Robert, but that's a whole heap of writin' ta git done in a week."

He chuckled and patted the top of the folder. "I wouldn't worry about that, Granny. We have a copy machine at the hospital and it will make short work of this impressive stack of papers."

"It don't surprise me one bit, Mamie added. You ought to see all the fancy equipment they have at the hospital, Granny. They've got so much fancy stuff, it would make your head swim."

Granny chuckled, and took another swallow of coffee. "It sounds right interestin', Mamie, but I hain't never been ta a hospital an' don't plan on makin' the trip any time soon. I've got everythin' I needs right here in the holler." She set her cup down and looked about the small cabin, her eyes resting on the wall of pictures. "I've got all of my kids over there, plenty of good food to eat, the best water in the world to drink and a holler full of folks to share my life and healin' with. What more could an old woman ever want?"

I've been meaning to ask you about all of the children's pictures," Robert said. "You just called them your kids. Other than Hillard, are the rest of them yours?"

Granny shook her head from side-to-side and let out a loud laugh. "Lord no, Robert! I hain't never been married," she said, in between fits of laughter. "Them children is the ones I has helped bring inta the world. I have more pictures in my bedroom, if ya care ta take a look."

Mamie gave him a look of disbelief. "Robert, you didn't really think all of them kids were hers, did you?"

Robert lowered his eyes, a sheepish grin on his face. "Well, I did have my doubts, but being back in the mountains. . ."

Granny wiped the tears from her cheeks with the corner of her apron, laid her hand on his and patted it gently. "That's ok, Robert. How was ya ta know anythin' 'bout that, with this bein' our first git tagether. The truth of the matter is, I fell head-over-heals in love with a feller who come ta visit some of his kin, back here in the holler. We took a shine ta one another right off. We was both nineteen at the time when he proposed marriage ta me. I accepted his proposal, and we set the date when we was goin' ta get hitched." She stopped to swallow the lump in her throat. "Three weeks afore the wedding, he was workin' at his job in the coal mine, when a huge piece of roof slate fell on him. It killed him right on the spot."

Robert watched as she looked down at her lap and fidgeted with her apron. When she raised her head, he could see a heavy sadness in her tired eyes. "I'm truly sorry to hear that," he said. "The pain of losing a loved one is never easy."

She sat upright in her chair and offered a half smile. "It was a long time ago, but I will never forget what we had back then. I tucked my sorrow into a safe place an' threw myself headlong inta the healin' of the folks hear 'bouts and deliverin' a whole heap of babies. I watched most of them grow up. Some has left the holler an' then there are those such as Hillard, who has made himself a good life right here."

Mamie, who had listened quietly, perked up at the mention of Hillard. "We can't forget old Hillard, now, can we? Remember the day he was born, Granny?"

Granny's eyes lit up. "Yep, he was the biggest baby I ever had ta deliver. He was always head and shoulders above all of the kids at the old school house. He was smart, too." She caught Robert eyeing the plate of biscuits. "Lord, where is my manners? Robert, ya best git yerself some more of them biscuits an' jam, afore they go ta waste."

Robert threw up his arms in protest. "I really shouldn't, Granny." He patted his belly. "I'm pretty full, but they sure are tasty." Granny raised one eyebrow, grinned, and nudged the plate a little closer to him.

"Well, maybe just one more," he said, as he quickly split it open and spread a thick layer of jam on both halves.

In between mouthfuls of biscuit, Robert let Granny's story tumble around in his head. With the last bite eaten, he brushed the crumbs off his lap and asked, "I've been wondering how you came about the name, Granny, everyone calls you, if you never married and had no children of your own?"

She smiled and let out a low chuckle, as her eyes roamed about the cabin and settled on a distant spot, only she could see. The memory of that day so many years ago, surfaced from the deep recesses of her mind. The feeling of pride welled up within her when the honor of being proclaimed a granny was bestowed upon her. Her smile widened, as the moment subsided. She folded her hands and placed them on the table. She looked at Robert and then Mamie. "Robert, my given name is Sarah Sadie Harris. I was always called Sarah while I was growin' up. When Maw passed on, I took over the position as Healer of the holler. Well, as the years passed, the number of babies I delivered was mountin' up right fast. I treated each an' ever one of them babies as my own an' still do ta this day. One day, while I was out treatin' one of the little ones for a bad cough, the woman of the house looked me in the eye and said, "Ya know, Sarah, ya treat all of the kids in the holler as if ya was their Granny. I think that title would fit ya jest fine an' that's what I'm gonna call ya." It didn't take long for the word to spread and I have been called Granny ever since."

Mamie reached over and placed her hand on Granny's. "It's been such a long time since I heard the name Sarah, I plumb forgot all 'bout it until you mentioned it," she patted Granny's hand affectionately. "Whether you are called Sarah or Granny, you are a great friend to many and a wonderful, carin' woman. I'm proud to be your kin."

Robert swallowed a lump in his throat. "That was a beautiful story, Granny, and a very nice tribute, Mamie. It is a pleasure to be in the company of the two of you." He paused for a second, as something Granny had said aroused his curiosity. "Granny, you mentioned you were treating the child for a cough. It has been my experience as a doctor, that most modern medicines don't work that well in controlling a severe cough. How did you treat the child, and how well did it work?"

She reached over and pulled her folder of remedies in front of her, licked her finger and leafed through several pages until she found the one she wanted. She placed the dog-eared page in front of him. "Ya can see by the looks of the page, that it has been used a whole bunch over the years. I don't rightly know who came up with the poultice, but it does the trick." She looked over her spectacles at Mamie. "Hain't that right, Mamie?"

Mamie thought back to the days when she was a young girl and the fragrant smell of the poultice that had been pinned to her nightgown. A smile creased her lips as the memory blossomed and the tantalizing odor filled her senses. "How could I ever forget, Granny? Them poultices cured my cough in no time and the best part was they made me smell like a fresh-baked apple pie."

Robert looked up from the page in front of him, as Mamie mentioned apple pie, and grinned. If this poultice works as good as you say it does, I'm going to try it on some of my patients. Who wouldn't mind smelling like an apple pie?" He laughed.

Granny pointed to the bottom of the page. "Ya can read right here, that onced ya place the right amount of cloves, allspice, cinnamon an' dry mustard between the squares of cloth, ya sew them up nice and tight. Ya then smear a good amount of lard on both sides an' steam them over a pot of boilin' water. When they is warm ta the touch, pin one poultice ta the front of yer shirt an' one ta the back. Ya will sleep like a baby right through the night."

Mamie pushed herself back from the table. "I'm going to rid up the table, Granny. I do believe we should be headin' up the holler to the Holcomb place. I 'spect Robert is anxious to see how Alma Lee is gettin' along." At the mention of Alma Lee's name, Robert's head jerked up, his eyes alert and a broad smile filled his face. "That's just what I thought," she said. She headed to the sink, shaking her head and talking to herself, "Lordy, Lordy!"

Granny's gaze followed Mamie to the sink. She was puzzled by her comments, but gave it no further thought. She turned to Robert. "Ya best put that folder in yer poke an' take it with ya. I spect I can git along well enough 'til ya bring it back. Ya have ta know that I don't use some of the old time remedies anymore."

"Such as what?" he asked.

"Well, back when a body had a headache, we'd brew up some willow bark tea fer that. Onct the settlement got ta goin' out in the valley, we could git our hands on stuff such as aspirin and the like. There is still plenty of natural plants that do the job just fine and we stick with them. Ya take a big mess of ramps and cook them up. They is mighty tasty ta eat an' the best spring tonic ta clean out yer bowels. There's yellowroot, sang (ginseng), chamomile, snakeroot an' a whole heap of other plants growing wild right here in the mountains. There are those who collect a lot of this stuff an' sells it ta help make ends meet. Shoot! A pound of dried sang can fetch up ta sixty-five dollars. Now, if ya want ta ask more questions, we best do it on the way ta the Holcomb's place. It's 'bout a mile up the holler an' the mornin' is gittin' shy."

Mamie had rinsed the dishes and set them aside to dry. She watched Granny struggle to stand, with Robert's help. "Granny, how about I take Robert with me, and we'll go out to the barn and saddle up the mule."

"Sounds good ta me, Mamie, 'cause my legs is 'bout ta give out, anyway."

Mamie stepped onto the porch and looked back. "Come on, Robert, you don't want to disappoint Alma Lee, do you? I hope you don't mind walking. Granny's mule can only carry the two of us old women, and that's a stretch for the poor old thing.

Robert hurried to catch up. "I don't mind walking, Mamie. Besides, I need to work off all of the biscuits I ate."

Just before she entered the small barn, she glanced back. "Yes you do, Robert, you surely do." She snickered as she grabbed the harness.

Robert's thoughts were not on the mule, but what lay ahead at the end of their journey, one short mile further up the hollow.

Chapter 18

Alma Lee sat on the corner of their front porch relaxing after a long morning of hard work. The warming rays of the mid-day sun soothed her aching muscles as they filtered through the canopy of the trees surrounding the cabin. She watched quietly as Jacob split firewood for the long winter ahead. She couldn't help but notice how much her brother had changed over the past year and since they had returned to the hollow. He looked as if he'd grown almost a foot taller, which would put him slightly over six feet. All the hard work he did to keep them in firewood, along with his many daily chores, had developed his muscles. He was lean and strong. His shoulders were wide, his waist narrow. The muscles in his darkly-tanned forearms were finely etched and the sweat that glistened on them only added to their definition. She watched him with admiration as he toiled. She couldn't help but think that some day, this blue-eyed brother of hers, with his light-brown hair, would move on to manhood, marry and possibly move away. Who wouldn't want to marry him? He was one handsome young man, quick to smile and laugh. He was, after all, a Holcomb.

At that very moment, Alma Lee wished with every fiber of her being that Maw and Paw could see their young son all growed up into the fine, strapping young man he had become. She knew in her heart that they couldn't help but be proud.

The ring of steel on steel grew dim as Alma Lee studied her calloused hands and picked at the dirt that was lodged under her ragged nails. Without warning, her shoulders sagged and a flood of tears poured down her cheeks. In between sobs, she looked to the near mountain ridge and whispered, "Lord, I'm so durn tired. I knowed ya has given me an' Jacob the strength ta carry on an' make a life fer ourselves, but right 'bout now, I shore do miss Maw an' Paw. It hain't been easy these past years, but we is still here in the holler, an' that's a blessing an' a comfort ta me."

Alma Lee swiped at the rivulets of salty tears with the back of her hand and stared aimlessly out across the small creek that flowed nearby and into the forest beyond.

A surge of melancholy washed over her as the soothing warmth of the sun eased her sorrow. With her mind clear and at ease, she recalled the day when her paw fetched Granny to help with the birthing of the baby. That was a day she would never forget.

It had been near Alma Lee's fourth birthday. Granny shooed Paw and her out of the cabin. Paw sat on the corner of the porch with a piece of grass clenched in his teeth, looking quietly out over their garden patch. Alma Lee walked closer to see what he was staring at. He picked her up and set her on his lap. He wrapped his muscular arms around her and held her tight against his warm body.

Alma Lee sat perfectly still as he pointed out all of the brightly colored birds that flitted about the garden and the nearby woods.

Just as Alma Lee spotted a robin that had pulled a worm from the garden, they heard her maw cry out. Paw whispered in her ear, "Don't ya worry none Alma Lee, everythin' will be alright." He gave her a reassuring squeeze.

As the noise inside the cabin settled down, Paw commenced to tell her about how it was for him growing up in the hollow as a little boy. Paw pointed at the little crick that ran through their property. "Ya see that crick, Alma Lee? I twern't much bigger than ya is now, an' I would wade inta the cool water clean up ta my knees. My paw, yer papaw, taught me how ta pick them flat rocks offa the crick bottom, careful like, in search of crawdads. Ya had ta be right quick afore they swam away ta hide agin. They's got some sharp pinchers on them too. So ya has ta pick em up careful like."

Alma Lee looked up at him. "Did they pinch ya Paw?

"Yep, onct or twict, but I learnt how ta do it right off, in no time atall."

Alma Lee laughed and squirmed in her paw's lap as he pretended to be bitten by a crawdad. He shook his hand violently and hollered out, "Let go of my finger ya consarned critter!" Then reached down and pretended to pinch her legs and tickled her in the ribs at the same time.

Once her paw had quit tickling her, Alma Lee managed to stop laughing. Breathlessly she asked, "What did ya do with them critters, Paw?"

"Well now, my paw would git a big pot a water ta boilin' an' drop them in an' in no time atall, they would cook up an' turn bright red. Paw would fish them crawdads out an' set ta shuckin' the meat outta the tails. He'd splash a little hot sauce on them an' pop em right in his mouth. He smiled wide as the first one went down an' licked his lips as he shucked one fer me. They was nice an' sweet like an' I could see why he liked them so. I likes them right to this day an' puts hot sauce on them, just like my paw did."

The more her paw talked about them crawdads, the more excited Alma Lee got. She knew right then and there that she just had to learn how to catch some of them crawdads and blurted out, "Would ya show me how ta catch em, Paw? Would ya, please?"

Paw laughed. He was about to speak when they heard a loud slap followed by the piercing cry of a baby. Alma Lee looked up at Paw with a worried look on her face. Her concern faded as the grin on his face widened and he gave her a reassuring hug and kissed her on the forehead.

Within a few short minutes, the door to the cabin opened and Granny stepped onto the porch drying her hands and arms on an old towel. She broke into a big smile and hooked her thumb toward the open doorway. "The both of ya can go on in." Then walked over to Paw and put her arm on his shoulder. "Winfred, ya has got yerself a fine baby boy." She then reached out, patted Alma Lee on the head and bent down to look her in the eye. She gave her a warm smile and said, "Alma Lee, darling, ya has got yerself a baby brother."

Alma Lee clutched her paw's hand tight as they entered the cabin and walked to the open doorway of the bedroom. There, propped up against a stack of pillows was her maw. Maw's face beamed with pride. Cradled in her maw's arms was her new baby brother.

Without warning, Paw picked Alma Lee up and set her down in the bed next to her maw. Maw put her arm around her and pulled her tight. "Alma Lee, this here is yer baby brother, Jacob. Yer paw and I favor the name an' that's what it will be."

Paw walked around the bed, knelt next to his wife, slid his arm around her and gave her a gentle kiss. "You did real good, Grace."

She smiled, looking first at the baby, then at Alma Lee. She turned to face him. "We did real good, Winfred." She reached over and placed Jacob into Alma Lee's lap. In a low voice she explained to Alma Lee how to hold her baby brother. Then she leaned back into the comfort of her husband's warm body. They both watched with pride as Alma Lee tentatively took hold of the baby's tiny hands. As Alma Lee's smile broadened, she looked up at her parents. "His little hands are perfect an' they is real warm an' soft like." Before she knew it, Jacob pulled one of his hands free and latched onto one of her fingers and held on tight. "Look Maw, baby Jacob likes me!"

Laughter filled the small bedroom, as Winfred and Grace soaked in the sight of their two children, locked tight together.

Alma Lee felt a smile tug at the corner of her mouth as she remembered the warm feeling of Jacob's tiny hand clutched around her finger, so many years ago. The memory faded, as a single cloud shuttered out the warming rays of the sun for a few short minutes, casting an eerie coolness over her. Those minutes were enough to change her mood and thoughts.

Breakfast was over. Jacob and Paw had gone out to feed and water the animals. Maw was washing the dishes as Alma Lee dried them.

Paw stuck his head in the back door and announced, "Grace, it looks as if the rain will hold off fer another day an' it wouldn't hurt ta cut down a few more trees ta add ta our supply of firewood. I spotted a couple of dead oaks over agin the mountain side the other day. I think we should cut em afore the wind knocks em down an' the rain soaks em through. I'm gonna hitch the mule up ta the wagon an' jest as soon as Jacob gits his kindlin' split, we is goin' ta head out. Would the two of ya want ta come along an' help carry wood, or has ya got somethin' else ya want ta do?"

Maw looked at Alma Lee. "Do ya want me ta stay with ya ta weed the garden? I will if ya think it's too much fer ya ta git done by y'urself."

Alma Lee wiped the last dish dry and placed it on the shelf of the open cupboard. "Maw, I think Paw would like yer company taday, so ya jest go ahead. I don't mind doin' the weedin' by myself. It gives me lots of time ta jest let my mind wander an' enjoy the peace an' quiet."

Paw headed out to hitch up the mule and load up his cutting tools. Maw ducked into their bedroom to change into her work clothes, just as Jacob walked through the back door with an armload of split kindling. "Paw said not ta fergit yer work gloves taday, Maw. He don't want ya ta get yer hands all splintered up." As Jacob dumped his load of wood into the wood box next to the cook stove, he looked around for his leather gloves. "Did any of ya see my gloves?"

Alma Lee gave him one of those sisterly looks and smirked "Did ya think ta check yer back pocket?"

Jacob snuck the gloves from his pocket and retreated, Red-faced, toward the back door.

Alma Lee grabbed her old, worn hat off of the nearby wall peg and walked out into the bright sunshine and headed to the garden with her weeding hook in hand.

She knelt down and started weeding right where she left off the day before. She looked up as she heard the creak of the wheels as the wagon rounded the corner of their small barn. Jacob and Paw were already on board. Maw hollered to Alma Lee as she stepped off the back porch and headed toward the wagon, "Ya jest take yer time Alma Lee. We can always finish up weedin' another day."

Paw reached down offering his hand to Maw, pulling her effortlessly into the wagon. He slapped the reins to the back of the mule and they all waved to Alma Lee. A chorus of laughter rose from the wagon, as it picked up speed, and they headed out for a day of wood cutting. Alma Lee shaded her eyes, waved back and chuckled at the sight and sound of her family as they disappeared into the woods. She smiled and continued her weeding. Little did she know that on this day, her life would be changed forever.

As the cloud passed silently by, she stretched and sniffed the air, remembering the sweet smell of the fertile garden soil and how it felt to her touch on that day so long ago.

Jacob was about to strike another blow, when he heard familiar voices float down the lane to their cabin. He put down the maul, retrieved his handkerchief from his back pocket and mopped the sweat from his brow. He pointed down the lane toward the advancing visitors. "Alma Lee, would ya look at who's comin' ta our place!"

Alma Lee, startled by the sudden shout from Jacob, blinked her eyes several times and eased herself into a standing position.

She turned and shaded her eyes from the bright sunlight. Sure enough, here came Granny Harris and Mamie, riding Granny's mule. Dr. Lane walked beside them. Alma Lee could hear the animated conversation among them as they pointed and laughed on their way down the lane.

As they got closer, Alma Lee stepped from the porch. "Hey ya'll! I shore am glad ta see ya. I can't believe ya didn't get old Hillard ta bring ya in his wagon. It's a right fer piece for Dr. Lane ta have ta walk from y'ur place, Granny."

The three of them turned in the direction of Alma Lee's voice. They waved their arms wildly when they spotted her.

Granny stopped her mule at the foot of the walking path and looked down at Robert. "Robert, would ya be kind enough ta tie the reins 'round that tree there?"

While he tied the mule up, Alma Lee hollered to Jacob, "Jacob, go on over and help Granny and Mamie down from that poor, tired mule."

"I'll be glad ta give 'em a hand. I was fixin' ta take a rest 'bout now anyway." Jacob helped Mamie off the back of the mule. Once she was safely down, he helped Granny dismount. Granny gave him a hug. "Thank ya Jacob. I believe I'm gettin' a bit too old ta be ridin' this old mule much longer. I don't know which of us is goin' ta give out first." With a chuckle, she slapped Jacob on the back and headed up the path.

Mamie gave him a big smile as she looked him over. "Jacob, it shore is good ta see ya again." She took a step back and tilted her head. "I do believe you have grown a little since you were at the settlement."

A wide grin creased his face as the blood rushed to his cheeks. "That's what Alma Lee has been sayin'. All I know is my trousers is gittin' a might short."

Mamie looked down at his boots and agreed, "Yep, they shore is." She turned and walked up the path toward the cabin.

Jacob turned to the man standing next to the mule. He stuck out his hand and gripped Robert's hand firmly. "Hi there, I'm Jacob, Alma Lee's younger brother.   Come on up an' have a set on the porch. If ya walked all the way from Granny's cabin, ya has got ta be a might tired."

Robert walked to the cabin, stepped onto the porch and headed straight to Alma Lee. He looked her in the eyes, smiled, and took her hands in his. "Why, Miz Alma Lee, would you look at you? You look like a different woman since the last time I saw you. But . . . those were different times altogether."

Jacob stepped around Alma Lee and hurried into the cabin and brought out a kitchen chair for each of them.

Robert grabbed two of the chairs and set them side-by- side. "Here, Miz Alma Lee, have a seat." He quickly sat down beside her.

Jacob had gone back into the cabin and returned with a large pitcher of cold, spring water and five glasses. He poured a glass for each of them. "I figured that y'all might be a bit thirsty after y'ur long trip here."

With everyone settled comfortably in the shade of the porch, Jacob sat down on the porch floor and leaned back against the log wall. He held the cool glass of water against his brow, sliding it slowly back and forth, savoring the moment. He couldn't help but smile, as he watched the people around him.

Mamie and Granny were engaged in an animated conversation. Their hands were flying this way and that way, as they laughed.

The stranger sat close to his sister, their legs touching. Their hushed conversation was interspersed with laughter, and every now and then, the man reached out and touched Alma Lee's hand.

Alma Lee had a girlish, care free look in the presence of this man. She laughed and touched his arm lightly too.

Jacob studied the man next to Alma Lee closely, as his own thoughts muted the conversations around him. *I can't remember if the fella told me who he is, or why he's with Granny. He shore seems ta know Alma Lee though. He ain't too big of a fella, maybe five nine or so. His hand shore was soft and smooth, but his handshake was right strong. He's got a right nice smile and his teeth are whiter than any I've ever seen. They's white as the first snow of winter. It's kinda funny that his hair is red, just like Alma*

Lee's, but gittin' a little gray at the sides. He kinda talks like Mamie, but different. Jacob chuckled to himself.

The sound of someone calling his name intruded on his thoughts. There it was again!

"Jacob."

He looked about to see who was calling him and spotted his sister looking right at him.

"Jacob, Whatcha doin' over there, daydreamin'?" Alma Lee asked. "In all of the excitement, I plumb forgot ta introduce ya ta Dr. Lane. He's the doctor who operated on me, and . . ."

Robert stopped her in mid-sentence. "Alma Lee, Dr. Lane is who I am back at the hospital. Now that I am at your home, would you please call me Robert? I'd like it very much."

She smiled shyly. "Shore, if that's what ya want me ta do. I think Robert is a right fine name." Then she added, "Did ya and Granny get a chance ta talk 'bout y'ur healin' an' doctorin' an' stuff?"

Granny spoke up. "We shore did child, and I was right happy ta share all that I knowed 'bout healin'. The good doctor, Robert, brought me an up-ta-date *Family Medical and Health Guide*. It was a fine thing he did, but with me gittin' on in years, I just might have ta pass it on ta the next soul who is willin' ta take my place as the Healer of the holler." A sad look crossed her wrinkled face. Her shoulders sagged a little more than usual. She took a slow deep breath. "I don't rightly know who it could be, but I shore will teach 'em all I has learn't 'bout healin' the best I can."

The mention of Granny's impending retirement came as a surprise to all of them, except Robert. Jacob was the first to speak. "Granny, is ya sure this is what ya feel is right?" She nodded her head slowly, in the affirmative, reached out and laid her hand on his shoulder.

Alma Lee was the next to respond. She swiped at the solitary tear, as it slide down her cheek. "Granny, ya was the one who most likely saved my life, an' I couldn't bear ta think of ya not bein' the Healer." She sniffed, and continued, "Has ya give much thought as ta who might take y'ur place?"

Robert cleared his throat. "Before we got here, Granny and I talked about this at great length. I believe either one of you, who are both young and have had regular schooling here in Winder Hollow, could someday replace her." He looked from one to the other. "Does that sound good to either of you?"

Granny chimed in, "We also talked a whole bunch 'bout the two of ya livin' in the holler all by y'urselves since y'ur maw and paw passed away. It's been goin' on three years since the accident. I knowed y'ur folks was protectin' the two of ya by not allowin' either one of ya ta leave the holler. But they is gone now, an' it's high time ya give the outside world some thought. Ya both have been out onct, an' maybe it wouldn't hurt ta give it another try."

Mamie sat patiently waiting for a lull in the conversation. Before anyone else could speak she took a sip of water and leaned forward in her chair. "Jacob, I don't know if Hillard showed you our school back in Cove Mountain, but if he didn't, I want you to know it goes all the way to the twelfth grade. I would be right proud for the two of you to come live with me. I have plenty of room and it sure wouldn't be a burden to me. Besides, I could surely use the company in my old age."

Alma Lee was the first to respond to Mamie's generous offer, "Mamie, I shore do thank ya fer wantin' us, but I is way beyond learnin' from more schoolin'. It's been a powerful long time since I finished the eighth grade, an' besides, I'll be turnin' twenty next month." She took a deep breath and continued, "Jacob thinks it's 'bout time I got hitched, an' learnin' how ta speak proper wouldn't hurt none, neither."

Robert turned his head to the side and waited until he was able to control his laughter. The memory of what she had told him, while she was in the hospital, about the way he talked, flashed through his mind. With a straight face, he turned to her. "Alma Lee, I think you talk just fine." He looked around the porch at the others and continued, "I believe I am the only person here who is speaking a foreign language, so to speak. I have never mentioned this to any of you, but I am originally from Michigan. When I finished my residency there, I decided a change of scenery would do me some good. I ended up in Fairmont. I had never heard much about West Virginia prior to getting here, but I'm really glad I made the move. This is one of the prettiest states I have ever seen and the people are the friendliest folks I have had the pleasure of meeting." With a sheepish grin, he added, "I suspect with the proper training, I can learn to speak the mountain dialect too."

You could have heard a pin drop as Robert waited for a response. It started as a low chuckle from granny and grew into a chorus of laughter from the rest. Their exuberance became infectious and he too, couldn't help but laugh.

When the laughter subsided, Granny spoke in a weary voice. "I hate ta throw a damp rag on all of this, but I is gettin' a might tired an' we has got ta git goin' back down the holler. I hope the two of ya give some thought ta what has been said here taday. I truly do."

Jacob inched his way up from his resting spot against the wall to help Granny and Mamie down from the porch. Granny held his arm as they walked to the waiting mule. He helped Granny into the stirrups and pushed from behind until she was settled comfortably in the saddle. Then he picked Mamie up and placed her on the mule's back, right behind Granny. Jacob untied the reins from the tree and handed them to Granny.

Jacob turned to shake Robert's hand, but Robert had not followed them down the path. Robert and his sister were standing on the porch, all smiles. He felt obliged to wait by the mule, considering the coziness they'd shared earlier.

"You know," said Robert, "I sure wouldn't mind coming back some day soon to spend a little more time talking with you. Maybe you could show me a little more of your hollow. It really is a very peaceful place. I can see why you love it so." He reached out and took hold of her hands. Then in a soft voice, he said, "I can't help but notice what a beautiful shade of red your hair is, with the sun shining on it." He reached out and lightly brushed a finger across the bridge of Alma Lee's nose. "Your freckles are delightful too."

Alma Lee felt herself blush--something she couldn't ever remember doing. With a gentle smile she looked at Robert. "I want ta thank ya fer those kind words. I hain't never had anybody tell me that afore." She looked down at the hands that were still holding hers. "I truly hope that ya will come back soon an' visit with me. I would like that a lot." She looked him in the eyes and smiled.

Robert's breath caught as he gazed upon the most radiant smile he'd ever seen.

Robert heard the mule stomp its foot a couple of times, saw Granny and Mamie waiting on him and knew he must say goodbye.

Reluctantly, he let go of Alma Lee's hands and slowly walked down the path. Alma Lee's gaze followed him every step of the way. When he had reached the mule, he turned and waved to her.

Robert gripped Jacob's hand firmly, looked him in the eyes, a brilliant smile spread across his face. "Jacob, it's been a pleasure meeting you. I hope that you will talk over Mamie's offer with your sister." He then added, with a gleam in his eyes and a sly grin, "you've got one fine sister there. I wouldn't mind getting to know her better." He looked up at Granny and Mamie, who were staring down at him with wide, knowing grins. He smiled and winked at them.

As their friends headed back down the hollow, Alma Lee walked down the path and slid her arm around Jacob's waist. They watched in silence as Granny, Mamie and Robert made their way down the road towards Granny's cabin.

Robert couldn't help but turn around now and then and wave at the two of them. He reached down and patted the neighbor's coon dog that had joined them.

Alma Lee and Jacob watched their friends until they disappeared around a bend. The only vestige of their passing was the settling of the dry dust as it passed silently through the sun's rays.

Jacob turned and took a good look at his sister. He looked at her as if for the first time, and approved of what he saw. There was a glow about her he had never seen before. Even then, his mind was at work. He couldn't help but wonder. *Maybe, just maybe, he thought,* as a smile creased the corners of his mouth.

Chapter 19

Cove Mountain, nineteen years later.

It had been a long, hard day of bone-weary work, and Jacob was in a deep sleep. He thought he could hear his sister, Alma Lee, calling him but her voice seemed to come from far away. He tried to respond, but instead, he sank deeper and deeper into the comfort of his sleep. The voice became louder and insistent. *Alma Lee, please let me sleep jest a while longer. I'm so darn tired from splittin' wood.*

"Dr. Holcomb. Wake up! Dr. Holcomb." His eyes snapped open. Standing over him was Ruth, his receptionist. Ruth had a wide grin on her face. "You were really making a lot of noise back here. I came to see what the matter was."

Tilting forward in his recliner, Jacob rubbed his eyes. A sheepish grin spread across his face. "Man! I really must have dozed off. Ruth, how long have I been sleeping?"

She looked at her watch, A little over an hour. You headed back here right after the last patient left the clinic. That was the last I saw of you." She paused for a moment, "you sure put in one heck of a long day. I can't believe how many patients you saw. I don't blame you for falling asleep."

Ruth cocked her and looked amused. "What in the world were you dreaming about? I could hear you all the way out at my desk. You were calling some lady's name I had never heard before. I believe it was Alma . . . something."

Jacob stood and stretched his lanky frame. He smiled pleasantly and began to tell Ruth about his dream. "I was born and raised, along with my sister, Alma Lee, not far from here, in a place called Winder

Holler. The dream I had was as vivid as the day it happened. My sister was very sick and we had to take her to the hospital in Fairmont for an emergency appendectomy. Our friend Hillard brought us to Cove Mountain in his wagon. Then Miz Mamie drove her from here to the hospital. That trip so many years ago, was the first time either of us had ever left the holler. Alma Lee was nineteen and I was fifteen. It changed our lives forever."

Ruth stood there in amazement at what Jacob was telling her. Her thoughts were spinning. Finally she spoke. "I have so many questions. I hardly know where to start. First off, where is Winder Holler, and what happened to your sister, Alma Lee? I've been living in Cove Mountain for only a month, and I haven't a clue about any of this."

Jacob gave her an appreciative look. "Winder Holler is about twelve miles north of where we are now." He pushed some paperwork back from the corner of his desk and sat down. "Several years back, the county built a new bridge over the river that runs between Winder Holler and Cove Mountain. Back then we had to ford it in Hillard's mule-drawn wagon. Now I take my four-wheel-drive truck back to the holler every week to check up on those who can't make it out to our clinic. I'm what the holler folks call the *"Healer."* Stroking his chin in deep thought, he continued, "About, Alma Lee . . . I'll have to give that some thought. Let me just say for the moment, there are two doctors in the family." He smiled slyly.

Dr. Holcomb looked at his watch. "Ruth, would you join me for dinner? We can go to the new restaurant that just opened up down the street. I could really use a good meal. We can continue this conversation over a nice glass of wine . . . that is, if that's alright with you? We could talk more about my sister and family while we eat."

A slight flush rose in Ruth's cheeks. She gave him an easy smile. "I would be honored to join you, Doctor, and . . ."

Jacob cut her off in mid-sentence. "Ruth, if you don't mind, I would prefer you call me Jacob. Dr. Holcomb works at the clinic, but Jacob is just Jacob when he is with friends and an attractive young lady such as you."

Ruth's heart skipped a beat. She knew her face had taken on a bright, rosy glow at Jacob's words. She took a deep breath. "Ok, Jacob, let's lock this place up and walk to the restaurant. The fresh air will do us some good." She really was thinking, *I don't know about you, but right now I need some fresh air.*

As they stepped from the clinic, they were greeted by a sky ablaze. Everything around them was bathed in the most brilliant hues of red and orange. It was as if the sky itself had been set on fire by the setting sun as it sank slowly below the peaks of the far-away mountains.

Both of them let out a slight gasp, awed by the beauty around them. At that very moment, time ceased to exist for either of them. Ruth and Jacob were lost in their own thoughts.

As the sunset paled, Jacob turned to head toward the restaurant. Then Ruth took Jacob's hand and looked up at him. "Jacob, standing here I have been giving your Winder Holler some thought. It sounds like a wonderful place to live. If you had to describe it in a few words, what would you say?"

Jacob stopped, looked down at her with a soft gleam in his eyes, the gleam he got when he thought of home. "I don't know any better way to put it than the way my paw used to tell folks where Winder Holler was. You know what Paw used to say?"

"No, what was it your paw used to tell them?" She watched as he stood a little straighter, squared his broad shoulders, and turned to face the distant mountains, the place of his birth.

Ruth's eyes followed his gaze and couldn't help but notice his wistful look and the slight watering of his pale blue eyes. He cleared his throat. "My paw would look right at that person, give them his biggest grin and say, *'Why, Winder Holler is back up in them mountains apiece, jest this side of Heaven!'*"

Ruth focused on the finely chiseled features of his handsome face. What she saw there was a compassionate man, a man at peace with himself, was proud of his humble beginnings and proud of who he had become. At that very moment, she knew that Jacob Holcomb was someone she wanted to get to know much better.

Jacob and Ruth walked hand-in-hand down the quiet street toward the restaurant. Street lights began to flicker on as darkness descended across the wide valley.

The restaurant parking lot was full of cars. "Oh! No!" Ruth said, "It looks like we might be too late to get a table,"

Noting her obvious disappointment, Jacob gave her a reassuring smile and gently squeezed her hand. "I wouldn't worry too much. They have lots of tables and I believe they will make room for us."

Jacob held the door open for Ruth. They walked into the subdued lighting of the restaurant. She looked around and slowly released her breath in appreciation of what she saw. "You were right. This is much larger inside than it looks from the street. It's kind of fancy, but in a good way. It makes a person feel welcome."

Jacob smiled at her response and with his hand against the small of her back, ushered her over to the hostess.

The attractive young woman standing there turned to greet them. When she realize it was Jacob, her smile broadened. "Dr. Holcomb, it's nice to see you again. May I seat you at your favorite table?"

Ruth looked up at him in astonishment. He reached over and slid her hand into his and gave it a light squeeze. Her mind was racing. *This is becoming quite a day. I wonder how it will end.*

Jacob smiled back at Ruth. "That would be great, Jackie." She pulled two menus from the storage rack and led them over to a quiet corner of the restaurant.

Ruth was impressed. The table was excellent. A crisp, white linen cloth covered the table. In the center was a lightly perfumed candle, glowing softly, casting warm, romantic shadows about. An overstuffed, curved, leather seat for two was behind the table. Two matching chairs sat across the table. Quiet music played in the background. *This is perfect,* she thought.

Jacob helped Ruth into the curved seat and slid in next to her. Jackie placed a menu in front of each of them, and asked, "May I get you something to drink, before you order?"

Jacob turned to Ruth, "How about that glass of wine I promised you?"

Ruth, feeling lighthearted, nodded. "I believe I would like a glass of Chardonnay."

"You might as well bring us a bottle with two glasses." Jacob said.

Jackie smiled. "I'll send it right over. Enjoy your meal."

Ruth looked the menu over. "What do you recommend? I gather you come here often, plus I trust your judgment," she said with a casual smile.

Jacob lowered his menu and looked into her dark hazel eyes. He couldn't help but notice an amused sparkle in them as the candle light flickered on them. Suddenly, he felt foolish for taking so long to answer. "I'm sorry Ruth. I was distracted by the sheer joy I saw in your eyes and I just now noticed the deep dimples you have when you smile."

Ruth was about to say something when the waiter arrived with the bottle of wine. It was perfectly chilled in an ice bucket. He poured a glass for each of them.

Jacob and Ruth nodded their approval. "Have you made your choices for dinner?" he asked.

Ruth looked at Jacob, and burst out laughing. "I believe we got a little distracted. Could you give us a few minutes?" He nodded and walked away. Ruth cleared her throat . . . "And your recommendations are? . . ." She placed her elbows on the table, cradled her chin in her hands and smiled up at him mischievously.

Jacob wiped his sweaty palms on his pant legs and picked up his menu. "They really have great pasta dishes, that would go well with our wine, or we could get outrageous and go for one of their mouth-watering steaks."

Ruth rubbed her hands together. "I'm really hungry, so let's get outrageous."

Jacob motioned to the nearby waiter that they were ready to order.

The food was excellent and the conversation flowed easily. Ruth hung on every word as Jacob recounted his life while growing up in Winder Hollow.

Jacob wiped his mouth with his napkin and leaned back. "That was a great meal!"

Ruth set her fork aside. "It sure was. I couldn't eat another bite." She looked over and spotted Jacob staring into empty space as a slight smile curled at the corners of his mouth.

"What's so funny?" she asked.

Jacob blinked his eyes several times and his face flushed at being caught daydreaming.

"I'm sorry Ruth. What was it you said?"

"I asked, what's so funny?"

He looked at her. "It was nothing funny, really. I got to thinking about my first store-bought meal, right here in Cove Mountain. The day after Mamie took Alma Lee to Fairmont, Hillard bought me a meal of cornbread and brown beans at the only restaurant in town. I thought I had died and gone to Heaven. Things sure have changed a lot around here, since then." He laughed and patted his full belly.

Ruth took a sip of wine and raised one eyebrow. "Brown beans and cornbread? You really must have been hungry."

Jacob chuckled. He knew what must be running through her mind, after the meal they had just eaten. He began to explain, "When hard times fell on mountain folks, food became scarce. In the past, hogs were left to scavenge the forest floor for acorns and chestnuts. This practice worked well to fatten the hogs, until the blight wiped out all of the chestnut trees. The number of hogs declined rapidly, taking away one of the staples of mountain living. Everyone had to make do with what they had the most of. If nothing else, folks could get hold of a sack of beans and some cornmeal.

The few hogs that survived were shared within the community. That way, everyone had a little pork to flavor their brown beans. To this day, it is one of the favorite foods of the mountain folks."

Ruth listened intently as Jacob unraveled the story behind his love for brown beans and cornbread. When he had finished, Ruth felt awkward about the way she had approached the subject. She was about to apologize when the rear door of the restaurant opened. A woman entered, gazed about and when her eyes met Ruth's, headed in their direction.

Ruth was mesmerized by the woman as she slowly made her way through the restaurant. She watched the woman stop at each table, say a few words and smile easily at some comment made. The infectious smile never left her face, as she made her way from one table to another.

The woman's natural beauty was obvious. She carried herself with great assurance and grace. She looked to be in her mid-too-late-thirties, with long auburn hair. Ruth estimated her to be around five nine with a very attractive build. She wore a dark green dress that complimented her hair.

Jacob, who had been reading the desert menu, looked up just as the women reached their table. He smiled when he saw her. She, in turn, broke out in a smile that accentuated the natural beauty of her face.

Ruth couldn't take her eyes off the woman who stood before them. The woman had the most intriguing set of pale violet eyes Ruth had ever seen. At that very moment, Ruth couldn't help but feel a twinge of jealousy.

The woman extended her hand to Jacob and in a soft voice said, "Dr. Holcomb, nice to see you again." Then she turned to Ruth. "And who is this lovely young lady you have with you?"

Jacob slide closer to Ruth, put his hand on hers and proclaimed, "This is my new receptionist, Ruth."

Ruth reached out and took her hand, as Jacob continued, "And, Ruth, this is my sister, Alma Lee Lane. She owns this restaurant."

Ruth felt a shiver race up her spine as his words sunk in. Her entire body tingled with excitement. Unable to speak, she stared first at Alma Lee and then back to Jacob. Ruth covered her mouth in surprise. She took a deep breath and managed to say, "Oh my God! I don't believe this. I've been asking him all about you ever since we left the clinic and now, here you are." She began to laugh and leaned heavily on Jacob's shoulder.

Jacob and Alma Lee couldn't help themselves. They, too, broke into laughter.

Alma Lee looked at her brother and in between fits of laughter, managed to say, "Jacob, you're still as mean as ever, keeping this young lady in the dark." She turned to Ruth. "Ruth, if you need to know anything about Jacob, you just come and see me. I have lots I can fill you in on."

"Don't you worry, Alma Lee, he promised to tell me all about your family and Winder Holler. I hope you will tell me something about yourself since you left the holler. You two have really had some kind of life." Ruth got a puzzled look on her face, as something clicked in her mind. "I just thought of something you said when you first walked over here. You called him Dr. Holcomb instead of Jacob. That seems a little strange for a sister to say."

Alma Lee laughed. "Oh! I do that all the time when we are out in public. Sometimes I don't know if he is with a patient or what, so I keep it formal until I know differently. Apparently, the two of you are way beyond that point."

Ruth gushed, "I sure hope so. Ruth said, with a twinkle in her eye.

Jacob flushed slightly, gave his sister a sly wink and smiled broadly.

Ruth had wished for the night to last forever. But with the last customer having left and the restaurant staff cleaning up, Alma Lee announced, "I hate to call it a night, but I have a ten-mile drive ahead of me and Robert will be waiting up."

Jacob and Ruth walked her out to her car. She gave them each an endearing hug. "Don't forget what I told you, Ruth, about coming to visit us real soon. I want you to meet my husband, Robert, and our two boys. By the looks of things, I believe Jacob will be more than willing to bring you out to the house. Now, I want the two of you to go straight home." She smiled and gave Ruth a wink that only a woman would understand.

Jacob and Ruth stood hand-in-hand as Alma Lee waved out the car window and turned the corner.

Ruth leaned her head against his shoulder and looked at him dreamy eyed. "This has been one of the best nights ever since I came to Cove Mountain. Your sister is so sweet and down to earth. I can't believe we spent two hours telling each other about ourselves. From what I heard, there's a lot more to tell, and I can hardly wait to hear it all."

Ruth gave Jacob a playful poke in the ribs.

"How come you didn't tell me that Alma Lee had married the doctor who operated on her?"

He looked at her with a playful smile and gave her hand a gentle squeeze. "Oh, I just thought I'd let Alma Lee tell you all about it."

Ruth stepped back, both hands on her hips. She gave him a steely look. "You've had this dinner planned for some time, haven't you, Jacob Holcomb?"

He smiled mischievously. "Yep, I've had my eye on you ever since I hired you. I'll have to admit I was hooked at first sight. I wanted to make sure the timing was just right. I can't take credit for the sunset tonight, but it sure was a great start to a memorable evening."

Ruth didn't know whether to laugh or cry. What she felt at that moment was pure joy. With starlight shimmering in her moist eyes, she reached up, put both of her arms around his neck and gently pulled him closer. Jacob hesitated for a moment, as he looked into the face of the woman with whom he had fallen in love. The kiss was all he had imagined. He gently lifted her off her feet and held her tight.

Ruth felt her tip toes touch the pavement, as Jacob slowly eased her down. Lightheaded, Ruth took a deep breath. "That was some kiss." With a schoolgirl smile on her face, Ruth took Jacob's hand. She said softly, "I need to walk, "Let's take our time getting back."

They walked slowly arm-in-arm back to the clinic. "I have a great idea for tomorrow," Jacob said. "That is, if you have nothing special to do."

"What did you have in mind?" she asked.

"Well, tomorrow is my Saturday to go to Winder Holler. I haven't been back for a couple of weeks, plus, I need to check on a fellow who cut his leg pretty badly. If you want to go, it would give me a chance to show you around the holler and our cabin. Besides, I want to visit the graveyard to pay my respects to Maw, Paw and Granny. What do you say? It'll be lots of fun."

Ruth jumped at the invitation. "I can't think of a better way to spend a Saturday. How about I pack us a picnic lunch and we can make a day of it. It will give you plenty of time to tell me more about your life." She took his hand and began swinging it back and forth as she hummed softly to herself, thinking about tomorrow's trip.

When they reached her car, Ruth leaned against the side of it and looked up at him with a sleepy smile. "This has been some kind of a day, Jacob Holcomb." And in a sultry voice, asked, "What would Dr. Holcomb prescribe to make it better?"

Jacob smiled slyly. "Oh, I believe I could think of something," as he leaned down and kissed her tenderly.

Chapter 20

At seven-thirty the next morning, Jacob pulled into the driveway of the apartment building where Ruth lived. The sun was cresting the eastern ridge of the mountains as he stepped from his truck. He watched the warming rays begin their slow descent down the forested slopes, pushing the darkness back for another day. Shielding his eyes, he searched the sky for any sign of bad weather. There was only cloudless, blue sky. His spirits soared, as he headed up the sidewalk, whistling happily. *This is going to be some kind of a day.*

He was about to knock on the front door when it opened. There stood Ruth with a broad grin on her face. She was dressed in faded blue jeans, a bright green, sweat- shirt, with a white collar peaking out at the neck. Her sunglasses perched on top of her short, light brown hair. Jacob, taking this all in at a glance, thought it gave her a smart, perky look.

Jacob took the picnic basket she offered, stepped back as he looked her over and let out a low whistle when he spotted the rugged walking boots she wore.

Ruth saw the look on his face. "What?" she said

Jacob gave her an appreciative smile. "Those are some pretty awesome hiking boots you have there. It looks like I've picked the right gal to go back up the holler with."

Ruth looked him up and down a couple of times. "By the looks of you, we're a matched pair."

They looked at each other and burst out laughing. Jacob took her hand and led her out to the waiting truck.

"You best buckle up, the road to the holler gets a bit mean in spots." Jacob snapped his seat buckle in place, fired up the truck's engine and said, with a grin, "Hang on."

At the edge of town the blacktop road turned to gravel and eventually dirt. Jacob's truck kicked up clouds of dust as they sped toward Winder Hollow. The day was ripe for two people in love.

The valley spread wide before them and the mountains loomed in the distant, but as they grew closer, Ruth threw caution to the wind. She unsnapped her seat belt and scooted over close to Jacob.

Jacob slowed the truck and slid his arm around her shoulders. He gave her a reassuring squeeze. "How's that, Ruth?"

Ruth snuggled into him with an impish grin and said, "Oh, yeah!"

The miles rolled by. Conversation and laughter came easy and natural as Jacob shared his thoughts about all he planned to show Ruth in Winder Hollow.

The breeze blowing through the open windows was heavy with the scent of trees, grasses, and the abundant wildflowers that thrived in the open valley. Ruth breathed deeply. "Ya know. I could get real use to all of this."

Jacob smiled. "Me, too, Ruth."

Ruth's thoughts wandered lazily as she pondered the possibilities of the day. She peered out over the nearby meadow. A veil of morning fog floated silently above the tall grasses. The warmth of the encroaching sun danced nearby.

Jacob slowed the truck as they approached the single lane, wooden bridge they must cross before continuing toward the hollow. He turned off the truck and got out. He walked to the center of the bridge and motioned to Ruth. "Come on out. I want you to see something."

Ruth slid across the seat, jumped out and joined him on the bridge.

Jacob pointed downstream. "See that big tree down there? That's where we used to cross with our mule-drawn wagons every time someone had to go to the settlement." His mind flashed back to the day when Hillard had taken his famous icy bath. The thought of it made him smile. He sat down and dangled his legs over the edge of the bridge. He held up his hand to Ruth and patted the wooden planks next to him. "Have a seat, we have plenty of time, and I think you'll get a kick out of this little story I'm about to tell you."

Ruth eased herself down next to him and began to swing her legs back and forth, as Jacob recounted the events of that memorable day. Her laughter came easily as he spun the dramatic tale of crossing the swollen river, with Alma Lee tucked safely in the back of the wagon.

When he got to the part about Hillard tying the rope around him, with special emphasis on how Hillard looked standing there in his shorts, Ruth burst out laughing. Afraid she might topple into the river, Jacob put his arm around her. Ruth wiped the tears from her cheeks with the swipe of one hand and held her other one across her stomach. Her muscles were becoming sore from laughing so hard. As her laughter subsided, she took a deep breath and managed to say, "Jacob, I'm so sorry for laughing about the dangerous situation you were in, but the way you told it was so funny. I just couldn't help myself." She leaned her head against his shoulder and tried to control another out burst of laughter. It didn't work.

Ruth looked up at him, "Am I going to get to meet Hillard today?"

Jacob thought for a moment. "We can stop and say howdy on the way to the cemetery. Hillard has a small sawmill not far from his house. He might be home, or at the little store we have in the holler. His wife, Emily, runs the store and takes care of the mail Hillard brings back from the settlement."

Ruth gave him a quizzical look. "That's twice you have called Cove Mountain, the settlement. I'm a little confused."

Jacob stood up, offering his hand to her. "That's another story altogether. I'll tell you about it on the way to the holler." He chuckled as he recalled the day Hillard explained the difference to him.

The morning sun flooded the hollow, casting shadows about, as they entered the sanctuary Jacob called home.

With the truck in four-wheel drive, Jacob pointed out all the familiar landmarks to Ruth. When they passed a cabin, he would tell her whether anyone still lived there, who had or was living there and a little story about each family. Ruth watched and listened silently as they drove deeper into the hollow.

About a mile further, Jacob pulled up beside an obviously empty cabin. Curled, brown leaves were scattered across the porch and piled high in front of the doorway. Gossamer spider webs hung limply along the porch railing. The sun's rays glistened off the tiny, teardrop crystals of dew that hung from the delicate, silky threads. A heavy growth of weeds had taken over the once well-kept lawn.

Ruth looked at Jacob and knew from the look on his face that this house meant something special to him. The slight misting of his eyes was a dead give-away. She reached over and lightly touched his arm. "What is it, Jacob?"

He looked away and cleared his throat. "This was the home of Granny Harris, our Healer. She passed away about ten years ago. The people of the holler have left it vacant as a reminder of the woman and her life-long dedication to the healing of all in the holler who needed her help. She was one amazing lady. We all miss her dearly."

Jacob put the truck in gear and was about to pull away, when Ruth said, "I think maybe we could do a little sweeping and cleaning up on our way back home. It seems like the right thing to do."

Jacob reached over and laid his hand lightly on hers. He nodded in approval and smiled. She had read his thoughts.

They passed many cabins scattered about the hollow as they drove slowly along. Some were built of hand-hewn logs, others had rough-sawn lap siding. All were weathered to natural shades of brown and gray from years of exposure to the unrelenting elements. Jacob pointed out one of the cabins. "See that one over there with the wood siding? We call that clapboard. It's easier to build a cabin with that than with logs. I prefer the natural look of logs myself. Wait until you see our place."

They passed women hanging out morning wash, men working in their large gardens or splitting wood. Each looked up as they passed by. They waved eagerly and shouted a greeting when they saw it was Jacob's truck. He smiled and waved back.

Rounding a curve, they spotted several young children wading in a small creek that meandered alongside the road. The kids shrieked loudly as they lifted rock after rock off the bottom, dropped them into the creek, playfully splashing each other. Now and then, they would reach down, grab hold of something and pitch it into a nearby bucket.

Ruth watched them intently. Jacob stopped the truck next to the noisy children. "What in the world are those kids catching?" Ruth asked, as she craned her neck to get a better look.

Jacob chuckled. "There're catching crawdads. I've caught many of those critters growing up. They're right tasty after you boil up a bunch of them and sprinkle on a little hot sauce. Kinda makes my mouth water, just thinking about it."

He leaned out the window and hollered out, "How many have you caught so far?"

Totally engrossed in their hunt, the kids hadn't heard or seen the truck. Their heads jerked around. "Howdy, Doc." The boy with the bucket said, as he tipped it up for Doc to see their catch.

Jacob gave them a thumbs-up for a job well done, waved goodbye and drove on, as the kids continued their search.

Ruth looked at him with an "I-can't-believe-it" look. "Yuk! You don't really eat those things, do you?"

Jacob gave her an amused look. "Yep. They go right good with a bowl of fried ramps, too."

Ruth rolled her eyes. *There is no way I'm going to ask what ramps are . . . no way!*

Jacob pointed at a log cabin in the distance as he negotiated a sharp curve in the road. "There it is," he said proudly.

Ruth stretched as far as she could to get a better look at the cabin he was pointing to. "So, that's where you grew up?" she asked. She tried to take it all in with a single glance.

Jacob pulled the truck over next to the path that led to the cabin and jumped out. He walked around the truck and gave Ruth a hand down. As they walked hand-in-hand to the cabin, he asked her, "What do you think of the place?"

Ruth was speechless as she took in the beauty of the cabin surrounded by brightly colored flowers. Beyond the cabin, a small barn was visible. A large garden was close by. From the front porch, she could see down the far side of the knoll the cabin was built on. There in the shadows was the little creek where the children had been hunting crawdads. She could hear the tranquil sounds of the creek as the water cascaded over the rocks.

Ruth released her breath. "Phew." A wave of peacefulness washed over her. She turned to Jacob. "Do you do all of the work around here to keep this place looking so utterly beautiful?"

Jacob shrugged his shoulders. "I always have plenty of time when I come to check on the ailing folks in the holler. Working in the garden, watching the flowers bloom and the vegetables grow gives me time to wind down from my life in Cove Mountain. Maw always loved her flowers, plus both of my folks worked hard to provide fresh vegetables to put on the table. There was always plenty left over to put up for the long winter months, too."

Ruth gave him an appreciative look. "I can see why you love it here so much. Now I understand how hard it was for you and Alma Lee to leave this place."

Jacob stepped onto the porch, swung open the cabin door and motioned for Ruth to enter.

As she stepped over the threshold, a different way of life opened up before her eyes. She was amazed.

Jacob had opened the back door to allow the cabin to breath. The fresh morning air swirled lightly around the inside of the cabin, activating all of the lingering odors. The sweet heady smell of wood smoke, infused deep within the log walls, was the first to greet her. As she slowly circled the large living space, she came abreast of the wood cook stove. Lingering there for a moment, she ran her hand lightly along the edge of the darkened cooking surface. The subtle hint of meals from the past floated nearby, and she absent-mindedly ran her tongue across her lips.

Lost in her own thoughts, she was suddenly startled back to reality, when the floor creaked behind her. Jacob had entered the cabin with a pitcher of water, fresh from the springhouse. He walked over to the sink and pulled two glass tumblers from the wall cabinet and handed one to her. "Here, I figured we both could use a drink."

Taking the tumbler, she drank thirstily of the cool refreshing water. "Hmmm! that is good water. Not like the chlorinated stuff we have back in Cove Mountain."

Jacob emptied his glass with one final gulp and set it on the counter. "I don't drink the water back there. I always take plenty of it with me when I leave."

Ruth set her half-empty glass on the kitchen table and continued her walk around the room.

Jacob headed for the back door, turned and said, "Why don't you take your time and look the place over. I'm going to see if I need to pull a few weeds in the garden. I won't be long."

Ruth barely heard his last words. She was engrossed with everything around her. When she reached the massive stone fireplace, she ran her fingers appreciatively over the dogwood flowers that were intricately carved into the wooden mantle. She could almost sense the pleasure of the woodcarver as he expertly removed each slice of wood. She assumed that Jacob's father had been the one who had done the carvings, built the cabin and laid the stone fireplace. She sensed that this was the work of a dedicated perfectionist. A man who loved what he did. Ruth smiled faintly as she thought about how Jacob ran his clinic--a dedicated perfectionist himself. *Like father, like son.*

Chapter 21

With a basket of fresh vegetables at her feet and two bouquets of flowers in her lap, Ruth leaned comfortably against Jacob as the truck made its way up the rutted road.

Jacob glanced at her with amusement. He playfully ruffled her hair. "Hey, are you still with me?"

Startled back into the moment, Ruth looked up at him and smiled lazily. "This is such a beautiful and relaxing place. I just wanted to let it all soak in so I won't forget any of it after we leave."

Jacob laughed. "I hardly think this will be your last trip to the holler."

"I sure hope not," she said.

Jacob gripped the steering wheel with both hands as he guided the truck onto a muddy trail that led into one of the smaller side-hollows. "You had best hold on, Ruth. Homer Poe and his wife live only a short distance further, but it gets a little steep in spots."

Ruth had already braced herself against the dash and had a death-grip on the window opening.

Jacob gunned the engine. "This is where it gets fun!"

Ruth paled. Through clenched teeth, she managed a weak, "Oh yeah, this is great!"

The spinning wheels kicked up loose rocks and the truck slid sideways as he jerked the wheel hard to the left and the truck swung back into the deep rut, just as they cleared a slight rise. There, fifty yards ahead, was Homer's cabin, high up on the bank above the road.

Ruth could see a man and a woman leaning back in their rocking chairs on the porch. The man's bandaged leg rested on a wooden crate. Jacob stopped next to the path that led up to the cabin. They both got out of the truck. Ruth carried the basket of vegetables from Jacob's garden. Halfway up the path, she looked up as the man gave a slight wave of his hand and said, "We done heard ya acomin' a ways back."

I'll just bet you did, Ruth thought to herself, but she smiled anyway.

"That's Homer, the fellow who cut his leg," said Jacob. He waved back and flashed Homer a smile.

Ruth, slightly winded from the steep climb, stepped onto the porch and set down the heavy basket of vegetables. Jacob stepped around her, walked over and shook hands with Homer. "How's that leg of yours, Homer?"

The man looked up at Jacob with hollow eyes set in a sallow face. His sharp jawbone was covered with the four-day stubble of a black beard flecked with gray. He glanced sideways at Ruth. "Doc, it's feelin' a sight better since ya give me them there pills, but its right hard fer me ta git 'round. I can hobble from the house ta the outhouse an' back an' out ta the porch here. I'm gittin' plenty of rest, but with me bein' laid up so and Pearl doin' all the chores, she's gittin' all tuckered out."

Ruth leaned against the rickety porch railing, waiting to be introduced. She tried to follow the conversation, but she couldn't understand most of the man's words and soon lost interest.

She turned her attention to the man's wife, who sat quietly staring into her lap, picking at something on her dress. Ruth couldn't help but notice how extremely thin the woman was. Her stringy, long hair hung loosely around her shoulders. The homemade dress she wore was badly wrinkled and in need of washing. Her broken-down shoes had seen better days. Ruth's heart went out to the woman. *I wonder how old this poor woman is? She sure looks like she's had one tough life.*

When the drone of the man's voice stopped, the woman ceased her rocking, stood and looked first at Jacob, then Ruth. She gave then a slight smile, holding one hand close to her mouth, to hide her missing teeth. "Would ya'll care fer a cup a coffee? I've half a pot sittin' on the back of the cook stove. It outta be still hot enough ta drink."

She hurried past Jacob and stared nervously at Ruth, as she headed to the open doorway. Ruth reached out and touched the woman's thin arm as she scurried by. She scooped up the basket of vegetables and handed it to her. "Here, these are for you, fresh from the garden."

The woman grabbed the basket handle, looked Ruth in the eye and nodded her head slightly. "I thank ya much."

Ruth noticed a glimmer of joy in the woman's deep-set eyes as she accepted the basket. Without thinking, Ruth stepped from the porch, scurried down the path and retrieved a bouquet of flowers she had left on the truck seat. Walking back up the path, she admired their simple beauty. *There are more where these came from, and I know Jacob won't mind picking a few more for his maw and paw's graves.*

Homer stared suspiciously at the flowers Ruth was holding, as she walked into the house.

"Is that yer woman, Doc?" he said.

Ruth felt a flush rise in her cheeks. She couldn't wait for the answer. She had flowers to deliver.

Homer's wife turned to look at Ruth as she heard her approach. She almost dropped the two mugs of coffee she held. Ruth extended the bouquet of flowers to her. A tentative smile spread across the woman's face. The woman mumbled. "I'm plumb outta canned milk. I hope ya an' the doc don't mind drinkin' it black."

Ruth laid the flowers on the corner of the littered kitchen table and took the mugs of coffee from Homer's wife. "Here, let me take them out. You'll want to put the flowers in some water. By the way, my name is Ruth."

When she turned to walk away, she felt a light touch on her elbow. The woman had picked up the bouquet. She clutched it close to her breast. A single tear filled the corner of her eye. "I want ta thank ya, Ruth. They is right purtty. I'm Pearl."

Ruth felt her own tears welling up, but swallowed hard as she walked to the porch and handed the coffee to the waiting men.

Ruth could hear rummaging in the kitchen and the pouring of water. Pearl emerged from the house a minute later, smiled at Ruth as she handed her the mug of coffee and sat in her rocker. Ruth noticed a slight change in the way Pearl carried herself and the tell-tale sign that she'd been crying.

Homer peered at Ruth suspiciously, as was his nature with outsiders, wondering what this strange woman had said to Pearl to upset her so. All the while, Pearl sat staring straight ahead, hiding behind her raised mug of coffee.

Jacob watched Ruth sip her coffee. She was watching Pearl out of the corner of her eye. A warm glow had settled over Ruth. He had the feeling that a bond had developed between the two women.

Homer coughed heavily and set his empty mug on the porch floor next to his rocker. He patted his bandaged leg. "Yep, Doc. The leg is feelin' much better. I 'spect I can git back ta cuttin' rails any day now."

That simple statement told Jacob that the man wanted them to leave. Jacob closed his medical kit. "The wound is coming along nicely and the stitches can come out next week. I'll stop by and remove them for you. In the mean- time, take it easy on that leg."

Homer looked toward Ruth, and with a flick of his hand, said, "Is she comin' with ya?"

Jacob looked at Ruth and gave her a sly wink. "I surely hope so."

Ruth smiled and waved goodbye to Pearl as she headed down the steps toward the truck. Ruth was halfway to the truck, when Pearl got out of her rocker, walked to the porch railing, and hollered out, "I truly hope ya come with the good doctor, next time 'round."

Ruth flashed her a bright smile. "I sure will."

The truck lurched to a stop in front of Jacob's cabin, startling Ruth out of her somber mood. She couldn't shake the image of a downtrodden Pearl. Ruth looked up at Jacob with a silly half-smile and laid her hand lightly on his. "I'm sorry I've been so quiet since we left Homer and Pearl's place, but. . ."

Jacob's finger touched her lips gently. "Shh. . . You don't have to apologize, Ruth. I understand exactly how you must have felt during our visit, and that's why I left you to your own thoughts. Homer and Pearl have not had an easy time. They cope with their lot in life the best they can. When he's healthy, Homer is one hard-working man, who loves Pearl very much. Both of their children died at a young age. Devastated by their loss, Homer and Pearl lost their zest for life. They've been holed up in that holler ever since, shunning most visitors. What you saw is the remnants of a young couple full of life. What you did for Pearl today with that simple bouquet of flowers was an amazing thing to witness. I'm so proud of you, Ruth."

Jacob watched as the sadness in her eyes vanished. Her furrowed brow slowly relaxed and she smiled. "I feel a lot better now that you explained it to me. But, I'm still a little worried about how Homer kept staring at me. I don't think he liked me."

Jacob threw his head back and laughed. "No, Ruth, just the opposite. He was quite taken aback when you showed up with me. He even told me you were right handsome lookin'."

Ruth shook her head, laughed and got out of the truck. "Handsome?" she said. "Come on, let's go pick another bouquet of flowers, plus I have one more question for you."

Jacob met her halfway around the truck and took hold of her hand. "Only one, Ruth?" he said in a tone of mock disbelief.

Ruth pulled Jacob toward the flower bed. "Well, maybe not just one." She giggled. "I heard Homer ask you if I was your woman. I didn't get a chance to hear the answer to that one. Plus," she said, as she put her hands on her hips. "I don't know if I like being called anyone's woman."

"First off, calling you my woman is just a local way of asking if you're my wife. No offense meant. Secondly, I told him that you weren't my woman, but I sure had high hopes."

Ruth watched the color rise in his cheeks. She cocked her head to one side, looked up at him and smiled. "High hopes, huh?"

Chapter 22

Jacob put his truck into four-wheel low as they forded the small creek that ran the length of the hollow. The sun was at its peak, casting dancing shadows upon the forest floor, as a slight breeze ruffled the leaves of the canopy. Ruth was spellbound by the natural beauty of the place. They made their way slowly toward the eastern slope of the surrounding mountains.

Without a word, Jacob stopped the truck and pointed off to his right. Ruth followed his gaze. Standing motionless in the shadow of a large tree, less than thirty yards away, was a doe and her twin fawns. Ruth took a deep breath and whispered, "They're so beautiful. How come they aren't moving?"

Jacob touched her lightly on the knee and whispered. "They don't know if we've seen them. They blend in so naturally with their surroundings, one can walk right by them and never know they're there. I saw one of the fawns move its head, or I would have driven right by."

Ruth slid a little closer to the open window to get a better look. Jacob, with a touch of excitement in his voice, said, "Look there! The doe is getting nervous and flicking her tail a little. She's finally figured out we've spotted her." The words had no sooner passed his lips than the three deer bolted from the shadows. Jacob and Ruth watched intently until the last of the raised, white tails vanished into the heavy underbrush. They turned to face one another and smiled as a wave of exhilaration washed over them. Ruth managed a breathless, "Wow!" Jacob just chuckled and put the truck in gear.

With the steep mountain slope in front of them, Jacob turned onto a grass-covered road that wandered off to the left. A hundred yards further, he stopped the truck at the base of a road that angled up the mountain side at a gentle grade. "This is it," Jacob declared. He grabbed the picnic basket from the rear jump seat and stepped from the truck. Ruth picked up the bouquets of flowers from the seat beside her and walked to where Jacob stood. Jacob took her hand and pointed at the overgrown road. "The cemetery is only a couple hundred yards further up on a large, flat plateau. It's nice and quiet up there, and the view is something else."

Halfway to the cemetery, Ruth spotted a growth of black raspberry canes along an old fence line. She reached out and picked a handful of the ripe berries, popped a few into her mouth and gave Jacob a dreamy look as the sweet juice trickled down her throat. Then she extended her stained hand to Jacob and said through purple lips, "Here, try some. They're yummy."

Jacob couldn't help but laugh at how young Ruth looked at that very moment. It reminded him of the days when he and Alma Lee picked the sweet berries for their maw. He could almost taste the jams and cobblers she made from them.

Jacob ate the berries Ruth offered. His teeth and lips now as stained as hers, he leaned over to Ruth. "How about we have our first and hopefully not last purple kiss?"

Ruth looked up at him with a bright purple smile. "How can a gal refuse such an offer?"

Jacob laughed and took her hand. Walking hand-in-hand, they reached the crest of the hill. Spread out before them lay the cemetery. Ruth stopped in her tracks and looked about in awe at what she saw.

The cemetery was surrounded by a wooden, split-rail fence. Tangled among the weathered fence rails, hung rose canes in full bloom. Blossoms of pink and red abounded. Their fragrance permeated the air. Ruth breathed deeply of their distinct scent. To her surprise, the entire area was mowed to an even height and no weeds crowded a single headstone. Wildflowers bloomed amidst the many grave markers.

Jacob put his hand on her shoulder and pointed to a corner of the cemetery tucked under a large sprawling oak tree. "That's were Maw and Paw are buried. Let's go over there first." He held her hand as they wove their way through the headstones.

Closer to the entrance to the cemetery, Ruth noticed the headstones were modern. Further back though, many of the graves had only slabs of flat mountain rock stood on end as markers. "Jacob, how come there is one tall stone and then a smaller one about six feet away on those graves back there?"

"Those are some of the older stones from back when folks first settled in the holler, some hundred years ago. The large stone marks the person's head, while the small one is their feet. Most of the older grave markers don't have anything carved on them."

Ruth nodded. "That makes sense."

At his folks' gravesites, Jacob set the basket of food on a wooden bench that had been fashioned from big logs, split down the middle. One half was for the seat and the other half formed the backrest.

Ruth handed him a bouquet of flowers, then watched as he knelt between the two headstones, removed the wilted flowers from the pottery vase, and placed the fresh flowers carefully and reverently in place. He looked from one headstone to the other. Ruth watched his lips move in silent prayer for each of them. She knelt down, placed her hand on his shoulder and kissed him lightly on the cheek.

Kneeling there, she silently read the inscriptions on each stone.

[Winfred Holcomb, November 25, 1920 – July 14, 1961] [Grace Holcomb, August 1, 1921 – July 14, 1961]

Ruth had done the math in her head, just as Jacob stood and offered her a hand up. Standing face-to-face, she couldn't help but notice the serene look in his damp eyes, a reflection of the peaceful sadness that filled him each time he made this journey home.

Ruth waited patiently. Jacob looked into her eyes and knew something was on her mind. A smile creased his lips. "Ruth, I can see it in your eyes. You have a question."

"I don't really have a question. I just couldn't help but notice how young your parents were when they died."

"I think of that often when I come here," he said. "Paw was forty-one and Maw was forty. They were so young, hard-working and full of life. It's been a tragic loss for all of us. I think about them often. I hope they would approve of what my sister and I have done with our lives."

Ruth reached up to Jacob and brushed her hand gently against his face. "I believe your parents would be right proud of ya."

Jacob gave her an amused look. "Right proud, huh? You're starting to sound like us mountain folk." He grabbed her hand. "Come on. Let's go visit Granny's grave."

The short walk to Granny's grave brought them close to the edge of the plateau. The view was breathtaking. The small creek shimmered in the sunlight, as it hugged the side of the mountain, wending its way toward the wide open valley a mile away. Several log cabins could be seen tucked back along the tree line with their patchwork of garden plots close by. Looking down on the endless canopy, they watched as several crows made their way noisily to the far ridge of the hollow.

Ruth, caught up in the moment, leaned into Jacob and put her arm around his waist. "This is one of the most beautiful, serene spots I have ever seen. Can we spend a little more time here?"

Jacob placed his hand on her shoulder, gently tilted her chin up and kissed her. "We can spend as much time as you want. Now, let's put the flowers on Granny's grave and then we can bring our lunch over here and sit on that big, flat rock over there. We can look straight down the mountain side as we eat."

Ruth turned toward Granny's grave. For the first time, she spotted the many flower containers that surrounded the headstone. There were a couple of old, Mason jars, three pottery vases and an old, brightly-painted coffee can with the simple hand-painted inscription, "Granny". One of the jars and two of the vases had fresh flowers in them. The flowers in the other jar and vase drooped lifelessly. Ruth gazed at the coffee can. She had a feeling that it was something special. She placed the bouquet into the can and arranged the flowers to her satisfaction. Kneeling there in front of Granny's grave, Ruth raised her eyes to the stone. "Granny, I'm Ruth. You don't know me, but I've heard great things about you. I can see from the looks of all the flowers that you're missed by all the folks in the holler. These flowers are from Jacob's garden . . . but I reckon you already know that, don't you?" She looked up at Jacob and continued, "I don't want you to worry about your place. We're going to clean it up for you."

Jacob nodded in agreement and knelt down beside her. With his arm draped over her shoulder, he reached out and touched the old coffee can. "You picked the right thing to put the flowers in. Granny, never having married, didn't have any kids of her own. She treated every child in the holler as if they were hers. The school children made this special for her. I believe a lot of the kids thought she really was their Granny, the way she loved all of them."

Helping Ruth up, Jacob said, "How's 'bout we go git that there lunch. I'm right hungry an' whatever is in there shore smells good."

Ruth laughed and punched him in the shoulder. "Talk about me sounding like mountain folk. You've spent too much time talking with Homer."

He rubbed his shoulder gingerly and said, with a grin, "That's another story altogether," as he headed toward the bench to retrieve the picnic basket.

The shadows grew longer as the sun marched steadily across the sky, casting the western slope of the mountain into twilight. Soon the hollow would be flooded in darkness.

The visit to the graveyard was more than either of them could have asked for. On their way out of the hollow they stopped to visit Hillard, but Hillard and his wife had left the hollow for the day. Meeting Jacob's friend is something Ruth will have to look forward to at another time. They cleaned up around Granny's and silently said their "Good-byes."

The open valley loomed before them and Jacob fell into deep thought. With his thoughts collected, he broke his silence. "Ruth, are you doing anything special tomorrow?"

The sudden question roused Ruth from her dreamlike state. In a sleepy voice, she asked. "What did you have in mind?"

"I guess I should have mentioned it earlier, but it slipped my mind until just now. Alma Lee invited us to come to her place tomorrow. She wants you to meet Robert and the boys. They're going to have a big brunch with all the fixings."

Ruth sat up straight and turned to face him. "That sounds good to me. Did she ask us to bring anything?"

"Just ourselves, but we could take a couple of bottles of wine with us, that is . . . if you'd like some?"

"I've a nice bottle of Chardonnay we could take," she said, "I'm really looking forward to seeing their home. Alma Lee said she would be happy to tell me all about what happened to the two of you once you left the holler. That would really make the day special."

Jacob turned on the truck headlights as they approached the wooden bridge. His thoughts were filled with the memories of the day and the possibilities of tomorrow. A satisfied smile spread across his face.

Chapter 23

The Sunday morning sky was slightly overcast. Ruth stepped from her apartment with her favorite ball cap on and a light jacket draped over her arm. Jacob had warned her that Robert and Alma Lee's home was high in the mountains and she should come prepared for it to be a little cooler than in the valley.

Jacob leaned against his truck. He beamed broadly as he watched her walk towards him. "Ya sure look right smart this mornin', Miz Ruth."

Ruth eyed him suspiciously and tilted her head. "Is ya goin' ta git started with that again?" They burst out laughing as he helped her into the truck.

Jacob started the engine and as they pulled away from the curb, he said, "We're on our way" Ruth snuggled against him and gave him a peck on the cheek.

Leaving the valley far behind, they sang a medley of songs as the truck eagerly raced up the steep mountain road.

Three miles out of Cove Mountain, Jacob pulled off the road at a scenic overlook. Surrounded by arched peaks, the overlook offered a view of Cove Mountain spread out below. "Every time I come up here, it's hard for me to believe just how much Cove Mountain has grown since the first time I saw it. I'll bet there were only four or five hundred people living there back then. Now look at it. Last I heard there were around six thousand and it's still growing."

Ruth's eyes followed his gaze, "It sure isn't Winder Holler, is it?" she said.

He smiled. "No, it surely isn't."

Ruth marveled at the beauty of the mountain views that changed dramatically with every twist and turn in the road. She scooted closer to the open window and stuck her arm out, flying the rushing currents of wind with her hand. "You know, I haven't done this since I was a little girl."

Jacob smiled at her. "You need to get out a little more often, Ruth." He reached over and tousled her short hair.

Ruth leaned against the window opening, admiring the scenery. "I could ride for hours up here and just let my mind wander, without a care in the world."

Jacob looked over at her. "If you think this is pretty, just wait until you see the view from Alma Lee's place. You'd best hang on, because this is our turn up ahead."

Once off the blacktop, Jacob slowed the truck. Over the noise of the gravel being kicked up, she heard him say, "Robert and Alma Lee's house is only about another half mile."

Ruth asked. "How far is it from Cove Mountain to their place?"

"It's pretty close to ten miles. Once they got married and could afford to have their house built, they wanted to be halfway between Fairmont and Cove Mountain. That way Robert would be close to his practice and the hospital and Alma Lee would be close to Cove Mountain, where their sons went to school."

The road narrowed. Overhanging branches arched over the road, giving it the look of a long, forested tunnel. Sunlight flickered through the thick branches, casting strobe-light patterns on the windshield.

Emerging from the dark tunnel into the bright sunlight, a breathtaking view greeted them. They were surrounded by acres of high mountain meadows. Tall grasses swayed in the light morning breeze. The gentle slope of the meadow gave way to a dramatic drop off that exposed the valley below. A ribbon of river wandered lazily through the valley floor. The morning sun shimmered brightly from its rippled surface.

Ruth drew a deep breath at the sight. Her eyes wandered slowly from the meadow to the river below and then to the endless parade of mountain tops that disappeared beyond the horizon. "When you said the view was going to be nice, I didn't think it could get any better until just now. This is beyond description."

"Look over to your left. You can see their house at the far edge of the meadow," Jacob said.

Ruth let out a low whistle "I thought you said they had a log cabin. I imagined something a little more like your place back in the holler. That sure looks mighty big from here. I can hardly wait to get a closer look."

The truck topped the last rise and Jacob turned sharply into the long, graveled driveway to Robert and Alma Lee's home.

Halfway down the drive, Ruth pointed out another large building a hundred yards or so behind the house. "What's that other building?" she asked.

"That's the horse barn."

"Horses, too! Where's the swimming pool?" she teased.

A smile split his lips. "The pool is just the other side of the house."

Ruth sucked in a deep breath, as he answered her off-handed remark. She reached out and touched his arm. "Jacob, I'm getting a little nervous about meeting Robert and the boys. My stomach is fluttering like it's full of butterflies.

He reached over and ruffled her hair. "Just relax, Ruth. You'll do just fine."

Chapter 24

Robert and Alma Lee walked arm-in-arm to their front gate when they heard the truck approach. Jacob and Ruth got out of the truck and Alma Lee hollered out. "It's about time the two of you got here. Robert has been driving me nuts looking out the window every few minutes, wondering when he was going to get to meet Ruth."

Jacob and Ruth walked slowly toward them, hand-in-hand. Jacob whispered something in Ruth's ear. She laughed. Her face turned a deep shade of red.

Alma Lee stepped forward and gave Ruth a big hug and shook her finger at her brother. "What in the world did you say to this poor gal to make her blush so?"

Jacob smiled. "I think Ruth and I will keep that one a secret."

Ruth poked him in the ribs, just as Robert spoke. "So, this is the gal that has finally managed to get this guy thinking about something other than medicine. I thought I would never see the day."

Jacob shook Robert's hand, as he placed his other hand firmly on Robert's shoulder and gave him a steely look. "I owe you one, Robert." They both laughed.

"Now, may I finally meet this lovely young lady?" asked Robert.

Ruth turned to Robert and stuck out her hand. Robert, without skipping a beat, said, "Darling, I don't shake hands with good-looking women." He reached out and gave her a big, friendly hug, several pats of welcome on her back and a kiss on the cheek. Robert sighed. "I've been waiting to do that all morning long."

Alma Lee gave him one of her looks. "Robert, give Ruth some breathing room. Are you trying to scare her away before we get to know her?"

"That's okay Alma Lee," Ruth said. "I kinda like the way Robert greets people."

"See there! She's smart, as well as good-looking," crowed Robert.

Alma Lee put her arm around Ruth. "Come on, Ruth, let's get you into the house before Robert talks you to death. I have brunch on the stove."

Ruth admired the beauty of the flower beds lining the split-rail fence that separated the house from the meadow. Hanging baskets, overflowing with lush blossoms, welcomed Ruth as she stepped onto the porch.

Robert and Jacob lingered behind.

Alma Lee ushered Ruth to the kitchen table, set for four. Ruth took in the simple, comfortable surroundings as she breathed in the tantalizing aromas that floated about the room.

Alma Lee heaped serving dishes full of the delicious smelling food and set them on the table. "Ruth, you can help yourself to a cup of coffee from the pot over there."

Ruth filled a cup, took a sip of the dark brew and set her cup on the counter. "How about I give you a hand putting things on the table?"

Alma Lee smiled broadly. "Thanks, Ruth. You're going to fit in just fine."

Ruth filled the glasses on the table with fresh- squeezed orange juice and set the chilled fruit bowls out just as the men entered the kitchen.

Jacob took in the heaping dishes of food and noticed that there were only four place settings. "Where are the boys?"

Robert spoke up. "They ate a little while ago and are out riding the horses. They should be back in an hour or so. I'm sure they'll clean-up the leftovers."

Alma Lee snickered, "You can bet on that. Now, everybody grab a seat and we can get started."

Ruth sat, took a sip of her juice and slowly surveyed the tempting dishes of food before her. *Should I stick to my diet? Maybe I can try just a little of everything.*

Pausing mid-thought, her mouth watered as a bowl of cheesy scrambled eggs were passed to her. *Forget the diet!* The scrambled eggs were followed by fried potatoes, sausage links, steaming hot biscuits, three different kinds of homemade jam and if that wasn't enough, sausage gravy for the biscuits. Ruth downed her tall glass of orange juice and dug in.

After brunch, Ruth helped Alma Lee clear the table while the men walked out onto the front porch.

Robert walked to the edge of the porch, leaned against the railing and faced Jacob, who had taken a seat in one of the comfortable rockers. "That Ruth is one sweet gal. I do believe you have found yourself a real winner, Jacob."

Jacob eyed Robert with a serious look on his face.

"I know, Robert. I never thought I'd find anyone like her, but there she was filling out a job application at the clinic. The smartest thing I ever did was to hire her, right on the spot. After working with her for the first week, I began to have feelings I had never had before."

Robert held up his hand before Jacob could continue. "It sounds to me like Ruth is the gal you have been looking for. So why the long face?"

"I'm a little worried that she will say "No" if I ask her to marry me."

Robert gave him an incredulous look. "Are you kidding me? From what I see and hear, if you don't ask her soon, I think she'll be the one doing the asking."

Jacob stood and walked to the railing. He absent- mindedly looked out over the mountains. "Do you really think so?"

Robert looked him in the eye. "Yep, and the sooner you ask her, the better."

They heard Ruth and Alma Lee coming long before they got to the screen door . . . laughing and talking non-stop. Robert and Jacob turned as they heard the screen door close.

The two women stopped short at the serious look on the men's faces. "What in the world have you two been talking about to put such a look on your faces?" Alma Lee asked.

Robert managed a sheepish grin as he nudged Jacob with his elbow. Jacob flushed a little but managed to blurt out, "Robert had just asked me how the clinic was coming along. You know . . . just a little shop-talk."

Alma Lee gave him one of her sideways glances. "Just a little shop-talk, huh? Well, enough of that. Ruth is dying to ask us a bunch of questions, and I think the time is perfect."

With all four rockers in a semi-circle facing the mountains, Ruth began. "Robert, the only thing that Jacob has told me about you is that you were the doctor who operated on Alma Lee. If you don't mind me asking, what was it about her that caught your eye?"

"Well, that kind of happened over several days during her stay at the hospital," Robert replied. "When she first came in, she was pretty upset and after I examined her, I gave her a sedative. Now that I think about it, I guess I was taken aback when she looked up at me from the hospital gurney, giggled, gave me a lopsided smile and told me I had pretty hair. How could a guy resist something like that?"

Alma Lee reached over and gave him a playful slap on the shoulder. "How come you never told me about that?"

"Hey!" He rubbed his shoulder, faking injury. "I forgot about it, until just now. I'll have to admit I was really hooked when I visited her in the holler for the first time. She was in her own element. The day was perfect. I'd never seen such natural beauty in a young woman. She was so full of life. I truly believe the peacefulness and beauty of Winder Holler is the perfect place to fall in love. She had my heart from that very first visit and still does." Robert placed his hand lightly on Alma Lee's. A loving smile formed at the corner of his mouth.

Ruth looked from one to the other and marveled at the radiance they exuded.

"I can relate to the feeling you had when you visited the holler, Robert." Ruth said, "When we were there yesterday, I felt so relaxed. The quiet beauty of the holler, made me feel right at home. I could see that it took a lot of hard work and sweat to make a living there, but that way of life had to be very rewarding too. I don't know if I would have ever wanted to leave such a place."

Jacob, who had been quietly listening, said, "We really didn't want to leave, but we had to go to the settlement because Alma Lee was so sick. Once we returned, Granny convinced us it was time for the two of us to experience the outside world." Jacob paused to collect his thoughts then continued. "I'd gone as far as I could with my education in the small school in the holler, so we accepted Miz Mamie's offer to live with her in the settlement. Back then the settlement had a school that went all the way to the twelfth grade. Miz Mamie enrolled me in the ninth grade shortly after we moved."

Alma Lee spoke up. "And I couldn't just sit around, so I got a job at the grocery store to earn some extra money to help buy groceries and a few new clothes for me and Jacob. The clothes we had on our backs had seen better days, and our extra clothes weren't much to brag about either. We could hardly live in town, looking like a couple of wood hicks."

A smile crossed her face as she remembered those days. She chuckled. "One thing that really made us stand out was the way we talked. Not that we thought it sounded strange, but the town folks seemed to have a little trouble understanding some of our words."

Jacob feigned a hurt look. "Did you have to bring that up, Alma Lee? I took some pretty heavy ribbing from the kids at school. Some of the guys started mimicking me, until I set them straight one day."

Robert laughed. "I remember those days. I thought you got the worst of it, until I spotted a few of those boys around town, sporting some black eyes and bruises."

"Now, if you want to talk about trouble," Robert said, "just listen to this. Not only was I accused of speaking strangely, by guess who . . ." he looked directly at Alma Lee . . . "but I had to promise I wouldn't laugh to much as she learned to speak a little more, like the town folks. Thank God she was a fast learner."

"Now, Robert, I wasn't as fast a learner as you thought I was. I spent many long hours listening to how folks talked while I worked at the grocery store. I worked real hard at using words such as 'haven't" instead of 'haint', 'just' instead of 'jest', 'sure' instead of 'shore' and 'once' instead of 'onct'." Alma Lee hesitated and took a deep breath, as the memories of those early days surfaced. When she finally exhaled, her shoulders sagged ever so slightly, as she lowered her voice and continued, "It's not an easy thing to cast off the mountain way of talking. The frustration I felt, as I struggled to fit in, was unbearable at times. I can remember crying myself to sleep many nights, but I wasn't about to give up." She swallowed the lump in her throat and turned to Jacob. "Those were some tough times, weren't they, Jacob?"

"That's for sure, Alma Lee. We grew up with how everyone in the holler talked and didn't give it a second thought. Alma Lee and I would spend hours coaching each other almost every night. We actually made a game out of catching one another slipping back into the mountain speak. One can never get rid of the mountain twang, but one can learn the proper usage of the words."

Alma Lee's somber mood was cast aside when a distant memory popped into her head. She burst out laughing. "Jacob, do you remember when you were in the third grade and I was in the eighth, and we got a new teacher from outside of the holler?"

Jacob pursed his lips and shook his head. "I remember the new teacher, but that's about all. Why? What happened?"

"Well, one of the first things she tried to do was to get all of the kids to speak correctly. It was her first teaching job and she was bound and determined to make us see the error of our ways. If someone slipped up, she would make us say the word correctly four or five times until we said it to her liking. Then she would ask, 'Now, isn't that better?'"

Jacob interrupted. "Yes! I remember that. And we always had to answer, 'Yes, Miz Taylor.'"

"The best part," said Alma Lee, "was the time when she had been teaching for about five months, and someone forgot their homework assignment. That really got her riled up. She stood up and scolded the little girl right in front of all of us. She was shaking her finger back and forth and finally blurted out, 'Elizabeth, did ya not remember y'ur homework, again?' The words had no sooner left Miss Taylor's mouth, when we saw the color rise in her cheeks and she promptly put her hand over her mouth. That set all of us to laughing. Finally, Miss Taylor couldn't contain herself any longer and doubled over with laughter."

Ruth wiped the tears from her cheeks and leaned forward in her chair. She looked at Alma Lee, then Jacob, who were doing the same. "If what I heard from Pearl and Homer yesterday is any indication of how you two talked, I can see how difficult it must have been for the two of you. I had to listen closely to understand even half of what Homer was saying."

Jacob interrupted her. "You should have heard her after we left their place. She started throwing in some of the holler words as she talked. She did pretty good with the twang in her voice, too."

Ruth shot back, "It didn't take you long to slide back into it yourself. You didn't know it, but when I was in the house giving Pearl the flowers, I heard you and Homer talking just like two peas in a pod." She gave Jacob an amused smile as she playfully gave him a shove.

"It sounds like the two of you had some kind of a day back in the holler," said Alma Lee as she gave them a sly look.

"I told you there was something special about the holler," bragged Robert. "It causes people to do all kinds of strange things."

Ruth stood, walked to the railing and looked out at the endless vista before her. She turned to face them. "I have another question. With all the beauty I see before me, and the quaint town of Cove Mountain not far away, what did your folks have against the two of you ever leaving the holler? Jacob, you told me about Hillard making regular trips to Cove Mountain and back. I assume there were others who did the same. There just had to be."

"To be honest," Alma Lee said, "we had a great life in the holler. Everything we needed was close at hand. There was a one room school that went to the eighth grade, a small general store to buy stuff we couldn't grow or make, plus a small post office inside the store. If Jacob didn't get a chance to show it to you, I'm sure you'll see it another time. Jacob, you be sure to take her to the little chapel that's there. You can't help but fall in love with the place, Ruth. It is made entirely of mountain stone and the high-pitched roof is covered with hand-split white oak shakes. The roof has moss growing on it too. Years ago they built the chapel in the center of the holler. It sits beneath a cathedral of tall pine trees with the creek close by. And we are blessed with the many rhododendrons that grow there. You will just have to see it when they're all in bloom and . . ."

Alma Lee's voice suddenly trailed off. Ruth noticed a slight shift in her facial expression. Ruth had no way of knowing that a faint memory had broken Alma Lee's train of thought. She watched as a slight smile formed at the corner of Alma Lee's mouth then spread rapidly across her face. The memory had blossomed fully within her. She stared happily into space.

"Alma Lee, are you ok?" asked Ruth.

Alma Lee blushed, shook her head and said, "Oh my God! I'm so sorry. I had a flashback that reminded me of the best day of my life."

"And what was that?" Ruth asked.

Alma Lee reached over, took Robert's hand and looked into his eyes. A tear of joy slid slowly down her cheek. "That's the day Robert and I were married in that very chapel." She took a deep breath. "We spent our honeymoon right there in Winder Holler." She squeezed his hand. "Do you remember that day, Robert?"

Robert looked at her lovingly and whispered, "How could I ever forget." as he placed his hand over hers.

Ruth looked at Jacob. Jacob looked at Ruth. Almost in unison, they said, "You two newlyweds are going to get us crying if you keep this up."

Jacob looked Ruth in the eye, smiled and winked. "Almost makes you want to get married in that chapel. Right, Ruth?"

Ruth nodded and managed a soft reply. "Yes." She turned her head away as she felt the tears well up.

Regaining her composure, Ruth hastily dried her eyes with her shirt sleeve and turned around. "You still haven't told me why your folks didn't want either of you to leave the holler."

Jacob stood up and stretched. He ran his hands through his hair. "I can answer that one. Maw and Paw witnessed too many teenagers leaving the holler for what they thought would be a life of adventure. Some did alright in the outside world, but there were those who fell on hard times. They turned to theft, drugs, even prostitution. It didn't take long for word to get back to the holler about what was going on out there. Our folks felt it would be best for us to stay in the holler until we gained enough knowledge and common sense to do better for ourselves. You have to remember, when they died, Alma Lee was only sixteen and I was twelve. We did real well by ourselves until Alma Lee's sickness. And that's what forced us to leave the holler"

Ruth put her arms around him and gave him a big hug. She looked up at him to speak, but he put his hand lightly over her mouth. "Ruth, I can see it in your eyes. Once again, you have more questions."

She tried to speak through his hand, but only a feeble mumble came out. Jacob laughed as he slowly removed his hand. "Only one more?" he asked

"I promise, only one," she said and quickly added, "for right now."

Jacob shook his head.

Ruth leaned against the railing, crossed her arms, and looked directly at Jacob. "Would you tell me a little bit about your school years in Cove Mountain and when you went off to college? That couldn't have been easy, coming from the holler."

Alma Lee and Robert sat quietly and listened to the younger couple's conversation, attempting to stifle their laughter. Alma Lee spoke up. "I'll give Jacob's mouth a little rest on that one, Ruth. First off, I'd like to say that I've been so proud of my brother over the years. He took to the new school like ducks take to water. Jacob was always a fast learner and read every book and magazine he could lay his hands on while growing up in the holler. He progressed so quickly in his schooling that they had no choice but to jump him a grade within the first few months. Even though he did odd jobs around town in the summer to earn extra money, he took summer courses to speed up his education.

I was still working at the grocery store when Robert proposed to me. Once we were married, I moved into Robert's apartment in Fairmont. It was a struggle at first, but I managed to commute to my job at the store and spend several nights a week with Jacob and Mamie.

One day, when I was checking people out at the store, I came up with an idea of how to make more money for Jacob's education. The store carried a little bit of everything, including a few bolts of material. A lot of the women complained that they could never get the material they wanted. They thought a larger selection would be great. Back then, most women made their own clothes and used the scraps to fashion quilts. The storeowner always gave them the same answer.

'Ladies, I just don't have the room to carry more material.'

With Robert's help, I found a small, empty building, only a short ways from the store and opened the "Mountain Fabric and Quilt" store. Thanks to our maw, I had learned to make my own clothes and we filled a lot of our spare time with quilting. The shop was an instant hit and I quit my job at the store. I still own the place, but someone else runs it for me."

"I know that store," Ruth said. "I've gone in there several times since I moved to Cove Mountain. I had no idea Jacob's sister owned it."

Alma Lee waited for Ruth to finish. "Jacob graduated with honors from high school at the age of seventeen. From there, with the aid of many grants, he enrolled at the university in Fairmont. Once again, he put himself on an accelerated program. He took all of the summer classes he could and worked part time."

Robert chimed in. "You think you have lots of questions, Ruth? You should have seen this fellow. He followed me around the office asking medical questions, one after another. I don't know which one of us learned more. He soaks up information like a sponge."

"You guys are making me sound like a super human," Jacob said. The color rose in his cheeks.

"I say, praise should be given where it's deserved. And you, my favorite brother-in-law, Jacob, deserve it," touted Robert.

Alma Lee laughed, "Robert, he's your only brother-in-law."

Robert shrugged his shoulders, a silly grin on his face.

Ruth, tired of standing, returned to the rocking chair. "That's one amazing story. I'm impressed. But I sure would like to. . ."

Jacob raised his hand in protest. "Please, no more questions today. I have one and only one question for you to answer, right here, today."

Robert had a feeling about what was going to happen next. He leaned over and whispered in Alma Lee's ear, "Watch this."

Alma Lee gave him a quizzical look.

Jacob cleared his throat, swallowed hard and lowered himself to one knee in front of Ruth. He reached out and took hold of both her hands and looked her in the eyes. "Ruth, will you marry me?"

Ruth's eyes opened wide with surprise. A feeling of light headedness exploded through her brain and traveled down her spine. She caught her breath. "Oh my God!" she said.

Tears of joy flooded her eyes and washed unbridled down her cheeks. She reached out and placed her hands gently against the sides of his face. She slowly pulled him toward her until they were touching noses. "Yes! Jacob Holcomb, I would be proud to be your wife."

There was no hesitation in the kiss that followed. It was pure and passionate. Something the two of them would remember for a very long time.

Alma Lee was as surprised as Ruth. Her mouth agape, she turned to Robert. "Did you know about this?"

Robert grinned. "We were talking about it when the two of you joined us on the porch. I gave him a little encouragement to pop the question." Robert shrugged his shoulders and grinned. "I guess it worked."

As the blushing couple embraced one another, Robert and Alma Lee encircled them, offered congratulations, handshakes, slaps on the back and kisses all around. Alma Lee hugged Ruth warmly and whispered in her ear, "I always wanted a sister. Welcome to the family, Ruth."

Both couples stood arm-in-arm at the porch railing and looked out over the wide meadow, still feeling the rush of the moment. Robert was the first to spot them, as the horses and riders broke over the rise into the lower meadow. "Look! Here come the boys."

The back screen door slammed as the two boys entered the house. Alma Lee hollered out. "We're out here on the front porch, boys. Come on out. We have someone we want you to meet."

One of them hollered back, as they rummaged through the refrigerator. "We'll be there in a minute, Mom, just as soon as we grab something to eat."

Robert piped up, "See! What did I tell you? Those two are always hungry." Everyone laughed.

The older boy was the first to walk out onto the porch. He was busy chewing a mouth full of sausage and had a leftover biscuit clutched in his hand. A minute later, his brother arrived, spooning fresh fruit from a large bowl. Ruth watched the two boys, as they stood side-by-side eagerly munching their leftovers. She couldn't help but notice how much the boys resembled each other. They both had a full head of red hair. The one she assumed was the older brother was almost a foot taller than the other boy. He was as tall as his Uncle Jacob. The other one stood eye-to-eye with his father. *These are two good looking boys,* Ruth thought.

Once the older boy had finished his biscuit, he wiped his hands on his jeans and shook Jacob's hand. "I'm glad you could make it, Uncle Jacob." Then he turned to Ruth and said, "Hi, I'm Winfred, but everyone calls me Win. I'm the oldest. Mom says you're a good friend of Uncle Jacob."

Ruth smiled at the boy. "Why, yes I am, I'm Ruth. It's really nice to meet you, Win. She looked toward the other boy and said, "And this other good-looking fellow is?"

Win turned to his brother. "Charlie, put that bowl down and come over here."

Charlie did as he was told. Wiping his mouth on his shirt sleeve, he stepped up to Ruth and shook her hand. "I'm sorry for being rude, Ruth, but I worked up quite an appetite riding. I heard you say you're Uncle Jacob's friend. Are you from around here?"

"As a matter of fact, I work at your uncle's clinic," she said, as she gave Jacob and the others a sly wink.

Robert looked at Jacob. "Jacob, You're about to burst at the seams. Are you going to give them the good news, or do I have to do it?"

Win and Charlie looked first to their father and then to Jacob, with a half smile on their faces. They anticipated good news.

Jacob held up his hand in surrender, walked over to Ruth and slid his arm around her. "Boys, I want you to meet your new aunt-to-be. She's agreed to marry me."

Win was the first to react to the news. "I can't believe you finally found someone to marry you. Way to go Uncle Jacob!" he said with a strong handshake and a slap on the back.

"Now, do I get to give my aunt-to-be a welcome kiss?"

Ruth wasted no time. She gave him a big hug and a kiss on the cheek. "You too, Charlie," she said, reaching out to him. The three of them ended up in a big group hug with Ruth in the middle.

Charlie broke loose from the group and turned to his mother. "Mom, when did all of this take place?"

Alma Lee looked to Robert and Robert looked to Jacob. Jacob gave him the nod. "Go ahead, Robert. I know you are dying to tell them every little detail"

"Now that you mention it," Robert said, "you boys just missed the big event. Your uncle knelt down right on that very spot over there, not more than fifteen minutes ago." He pointed to a spot in front of the rocker. "It was really something to see. Actually, the look on your mother's face was the best of all. I don't know who was more surprised, your mother or Ruth."

Alma Lee finally broke her silence. "I was surprised about this happening so soon. I just met Ruth for the first time at the restaurant Friday night. I had a feeling Ruth was going to be the one, by the way these two lovebirds were acting."

The words had hardly passed her lips, when a thought struck her. "I know it's a little early in the day, but I believe I saw someone sneak a bottle of wine into my refrigerator this morning. We need to celebrate this grand occasion." Everyone let out a loud cheer, and Robert headed for the kitchen to get the bottle of wine and six glasses.

Robert poured the wine and raised his glass. "I would like to propose an engagement toast to these two lovely people standing before me. Ruth, Jacob, I hope your wedding day is as perfect as the day Alma Lee and I became husband and wife."

Ruth interrupted the clinking of glasses and the good wishes, as she requested everyone's attention. She first looked at Robert. "Robert, that was a beautiful toast. I thank you." Then she turned and looked into Jacob's eyes. Her face radiated the love she felt in her heart. "Besides marrying this handsome fellow, there is one more thing that would make our wedding day special . . . and that would be to get married in the little chapel in Winder Holler."

Jacob leaned down, gave her a soft kiss and whispered. "And the honeymoon will be ...?"

Ruth blushed, looked directly at Alma Lee, and pointed her finger. "Don't ask," she said as she gave Alma Lee a sly wink.

The tantalizing smells that emanated from the kitchen floated throughout the house, as Alma Lee put the finishing touches on her famous potato salad.

Robert and Jacob had gone outside to grill the steaks.

Ruth, Win and Charlie gathered around the table on the front porch. Ruth sat quietly at the table leaning on her elbow. She listened to the two of them discuss their summer vacation.

As her eyes shifted from one to the other, a thought struck her. She reached out and touched Win's arm to get his attention. "Win, you said your real first name was Winfred. It seems to me that I've seen that name recently."

Win smiled. "You visited Winder Holler yesterday, didn't you? Did you go up to the graveyard?"

Ruth nodded her head. Then the light went on. "You're named after your Grandpa, aren't you?"

"Yep, and Charlie, or should I say Charles, is named after our other Grandpa."

Charlie gave him a playful poke on the shoulder. "That will be enough of that, Winfred."

The two of them laughed. Ruth was amused.

"Do the two of you do this often?" Ruth asked.

"Every chance we get," they said, as their smiles broadened.

"Jacob tells me the two of you are going to college," Ruth said, "What are you studying?"

Charlie was the first to speak. "I've already finished my freshman year at the university in Fairmont. Right now, I'm leaning toward medicine, just like Dad."

Ruth tilted her head and looked Charlie in the eye. "You look a little too young to have already finished a year of college."

Charlie laughed, "I guess I do, but Win and I both graduated from high school at sixteen, and that gave us an early start on college."

"So what are you going to be doing during your summer vacation?" she asked.

"Well, I've volunteered to help out at the hospital. When I'm not there, Dad said I could work with him at his office. I'll spend weekends roaming the mountains on my horse. You're welcome to come on a ride with me anytime you want."

"I just might take you up on that, Charlie. It sounds like lots of fun, but I have to warn you, I've never ridden a horse before."

Ruth turned to Win. "And how about you?" she asked, "What are your plans for the summer, Win?"

"I've got something really special going on, starting next week. Hillard, from up in the holler, is getting started on another custom log home. I'm going to be his apprentice. That way I can learn the right way to build a log cabin. He builds them the old-fashioned way, using nothing but hand tools. I'm hoping to get really good at it. I want to build my own cabin some day, back up in the holler."

"That sounds like a lot of hard work," Ruth commented.

"It is, but I love being out in the woods and learning the old ways of doing things. I would have loved to have grown up in Winder Holler, just like Mom and Uncle Jacob. That's why my education is geared toward forestry management and preservation. I plan on doing whatever it takes to insure that places like Winder Holler and its way of life survive for years to come."

Ruth could sense the commitment and excitement in Win's voice. "That sounds to me like a very worthwhile goal. How much longer do you have before you graduate from college?"

"Well, like Charlie said, we both got an early start, so I have one more year to go and I'll be done. Shortly after graduating, I'll turn twenty. I can't wait to get started on our project."

Ruth leaned back in her chair. "If you don't mind me asking, what is the project you have planned?"

Win smiled broadly. Just as he was about to answer, Alma Lee walked onto the porch with a tray of dishes and utensils. "You guys can set the table, while I bring out the food. The steaks are about to come off the grill. I can smell them from way out here."

Charlie took the tray from his mom and set it on the table. Win looked back at Ruth. "As I was about to say, why don't we wait until everyone is out here and all of us can fill you in about the project."

Before Ruth could say anything, Alma Lee appeared on the porch again. She was balancing several large bowls heaped with food. Robert, with a platter piled high with steaming steaks was close behind. Ruth took one of the bowls from Alma Lee and peered past Robert. "Where's Jacob?" she asked.

"We didn't know what everyone wanted to drink, so he's filled a small tub with a variety of beverages," answered Robert.

Ruth saw Jacob as he approached the screen door. She quickly stepped forward and held it open for him. He set the tub down with a grunt. "That shore is a powerful lot ta be drinkin'," Ruth drawled.

Jacob looked down at her and shook his head. Everyone laughed. He promptly sat down. "Let's eat. I'm starved."

The setting sun bathed the mountain tops in subtle shades of rose. The distant river glittered no more. The valley was shrouded in darkness.

The table was cleared and the family retired to the comfort of the porch rocking chairs to watch the remnants of the setting sun.

Charlie excused himself to tend to the horses.

Ruth looked anxiously around the porch, biding her time, waiting for a lull in the conversation. Several times she raised her hand, in hopes that someone would notice her anxiety. Just at the perfect moment she had been waiting for, Win cleared his throat. "Dad, I was talking to Ruth earlier and had mentioned the Winder Holler project to her. I think we all can see that she is getting more excited by the minute, just thinking about it." Everyone laughed. "I suggest that you, Mom and Uncle Jacob tell her all about it, seeing as how she's going to be part of the family."

Jacob took Ruth's hand in his and gave it a light squeeze and smiled.

Robert looked over at Ruth. "Ruth, I'm sure that during your visit to the holler yesterday, you saw a lot of empty cabins."

"Yes I did, Robert. Jacob pointed out everyone we passed and told me who used to live there, along with some facts about the families."

"Well, the fact of the matter is, a lot of the older folks have passed away and many of their children wanted more than holler life had to offer. Many of the people who left packed up their belongings and never looked back."

Alma Lee walked to the porch railing, leaned against it and looked directly at Ruth. "It didn't take Jacob and me long to spot the trend of folks moving to the cities. Many of them settled in Cove Mountain and the rest scattered to who knows where?" She gestured with a sweep of her hand. "You can see by the emptiness around us, that many opted to leave the mountains altogether. I don't know, but maybe they needed a steady paycheck or just wanted to see what lay beyond the holler."

Jacob interrupted. "Over the nineteen years since we left the holler, the decline of people living there has been dramatic. Now, there are less than one-third of the families that used to live there. Even though we live outside the holler, we never gave up on what it stands for. We spend as much time as we can maintaining the old home place, doing our part at the cemetery and tending to the needs of the families who are trying so desperately to hold onto their way of life." He looked over at Robert. "Robert could see how much this bothered Alma Lee and me, so he came up with a brilliant plan. I believe he should be the one to tell you all about it."

Robert smiled broadly, adjusted his position in the chair and began. "Once we all had decided that something must be done to preserve the way of life in Winder Holler, I knew it was going to be a long-term commitment on our part. The first thing I did was contact the Governor's office to find out what could be done legally and how to go about setting up a conservancy. I wrote a proposal on what we wanted to accomplish and sent it off for approval. The response I received was overwhelmingly in our favor. I was encouraged to apply for grants to fund the project. The seed monies from the grants, along with donations from many individuals, has allowed us to gain title to all of the abandoned lands and buildings in the holler. All that we have accumulated is held in trust until we are ready to put our plan into action."

Ruth looked from one to another, with an excited but confused look on her face. "And, what's the final plan for all of your efforts?" she asked.

"Ah! That's where Win comes in," said Robert.

Win looked at Ruth. "Remember when I talked about building my own log cabin? Well, that's going to be the first new cabin to be built in the holler in a very long time. We are going to open up a Living Folk Art Village near the entrance to the holler. People can come from all around to learn the old ways of doing things. We'll be teaching: log-cabin building, farming, pottery, basket weaving, animal husbandry, blacksmithing and much more. Everything that is required to survive in the mountains will be offered. We plan on having week-long workshops, along with an extended-stay program. The empty cabins can be used for sleeping and cooking. The really exciting part of the project is signing up dedicated families who are willing to live the old way of life, right alongside those who never left the holler."

Ruth held up her hand. "Wait!" she said. "What do the people who live in the holler think about this?"

"Over the years, we have kept in touch with each family and assured them we are only interested in preserving their way of life and nothing else. They all have this in writing along with our solemn promise. Their response has been positive from the very beginning."

"And who is going to be running this program?" Ruth asked."

"I will be the one, on site, to get it up and running," Win said. "That's where I want to live and raise a family and is why I picked forestry as my major. My studies, along with working with Hillard this summer building my own cabin, should give me the start I need."

Robert chimed in, "We know things will move slowly at first, but with a good plan and lots of dedication on our part, we'll accomplish what we set out to do. We hope many of those who sign up to live in the holler will have the knowledge and craftsmanship to be instructors. This would fill our needs plus provide extra income for them."

All eyes looked to the screen door as Charlie stepped onto the porch. "Charlie, we have been telling Ruth all about the holler project," Robert said. "Would you go get the plans you've been working on?"

Charlie smiled broadly at the mention of the plans. "Do you want all of the drawings or just the overall layout?"

"The overall layout will do fine for now."

"You know, Ruth, Win and Charlie have been a big part of developing the plans for this project," Alma Lee told her. "They've heard us discuss it over the years and as they got older, they were eager to share our dream.

The boys have spent so much time in the holler over the years, it's like a second home to them. They know and understand the way of life there and don't want to see it disappear. I'm beyond words to express how proud I am of the two of them. Win, for his dedication to the old ways of doing things, and Charlie, for his talent and enthusiasm in drawing up the plans for the project. He even did the architectural drawings for the new log structures. He is quite the artist. I'm sure he'll be happy to show you some of his work, Ruth."

Charlie walked back out onto the porch with the rolled up layout in his hand. Robert motioned to him. "Bring it over to the table, Son."

With the drawing spread out, Ruth's eyes widened at the size and detail of the drawing. "So that's what the holler will look like when everything is complete?" she said,

"For the most part," said Charlie. "I started the drawing by using an actual survey of the holler that located every cabin along with the property lines for each." Charlie pointed to the opening of the holler. He put his finger on the large structure shown there. "This building will be the Main Lodge. Here we'll have class registration, a small store with school supplies, specialized tools and books for some of our workshops. We'll have a small medical station for emergencies and last but not least, the only telephone in the holler."

"You mean there are no other phones or electricity, anywhere?" asked Ruth.

Jacob interrupted, "Remember, Ruth, we want to keep the holler the way it has been all these years. There are some thirty-odd families still living there. We've agreed not to interfere with their way of life. As you can see from Charlie's layout, the new structures are all located near the entrance to the holler. Most of them will have electricity for lighting. We're working on a way to use the creek as a source of that electricity.

The use of motorized vehicles in the holler proper will be restricted for emergency use only. A few of the residents have four-wheel-drive trucks, but most still use mules or horses to get around. They prefer it that way."

Win turned to Ruth, "Well, Ruth, how does all of this sound to you so far?"

Ruth reached her arms out to Win and Charlie.

"You two guys get over here. I want to give both of you a big hug. I'm so glad that I have been asked to be a part of this family and believe me, it's going to be one great journey." She turned to Jacob with a radiant smile. "This has been some kind of a day!"

Chapter 25

Winder Hollow, early October

Robert elbowed Jacob gently and nodded his head in the direction of the doorway. Jacob, intent on the entrance of his bride, missed the entrance of his sister, Alma Lee. Jacob looked over at Robert. Robert's face beamed brightly as he watched his bride of many years walk down the aisle once again.

Jacob looked anxiously toward the back door of the chapel. He wiped his sweaty palms on his pant legs.

Robert gave him a sideways glance. "Are you ready for this?" he asked.

"I've been ready for this from the first day I set eyes on her, and, Yes! I'm nervous."

Robert let out a slight chuckle as the foot-pumped organ sprang to life with the traditional, wedding march.

The entire congregation turned as Ruth stepped through the arched doorway of the chapel with her father at her side. She strolled slowly down the aisle in the wedding dress Alma Lee had lovingly sewn for her. The elegant white dress, with its accent beading, shimmered brightly as she passed through an errant shaft of sunlight.

Jacob gazed intently at Ruth as she and her father walked down the aisle. Several times, he felt his heart flutter and realized he'd been holding his breath. He willed his weak knees to hold fast.

The wedding march faded as Ruth's father paused at the altar. He choked back his emotions, before he had to speak.

"Who gives this woman to this man?" the preacher asked.

"It is with great pleasure that my wife and I offer the hand of our daughter, Ruth, in marriage, on this, her very special day."

Jacob and Ruth locked eyes as they turned to face the preacher.

The preacher looked out at the congregation, smiled and began. "Dearly beloved, we are gathered here today…"

The ceremony was a blur as Jacob and Ruth stared into one another's eyes, lost in the deep love they saw there. The final words, "I now pronounce you husband and wife," brought them back to the moment. They kissed for the very first time, as husband and wife.

The music from the fiddle, banjo and harmonica was played with great enthusiasm as the dancers stepped lively to the fast tunes.

Traditionally, the first slow dance was reserved for the newlyweds. Jacob held Ruth lightly around her waist. They whirled and dipped to the music, as the guests hollered out good wishes to the bride and groom. They never took their eyes off each other. The love they saw there was more than words could describe. Ruth whispered in Jacob's ear, "Did you see how many people showed up for our wedding?"

"There are other people here? I can't say that I noticed." Jacob said, with a broad grin. He bent down and kissed his bride.

Ruth squeezed him tight. "I think everyone in the holler showed up, along with all our friends from Cove Mountain."

"You tell folks that there's going to be a big party and lots of food, you'd best step back and get out of their way," Jacob said.

They both laughed at the truth of his last statement and hugged, just as the music stopped.

Ruth looked around for the first time. The tables were lined up along the edge of the clearing, covered from one end to the other with dishes heaped high with food. The two of them worked their way through the crowd. They shook hands along the way and exchanged hugs and kisses with their guests. When they finally reached the tables, they marveled at what was spread out before them. There were several sugar-cured hams, a couple of wild, roasted turkeys, a steaming pot of roasted venison, bowl after bowl of potatoes, half-runner beans and everything imaginable that could be pickled and put up in a Mason jar. Their eyes grew wider by the moment as they looked from dish to dish. Jacob spotted movement at the end table and motioned to Ruth.

They worked their way toward the table where Robert and Alma Lee stood balancing the most spectacular wedding cake they had ever seen. "Wow! Ruth, would you look at that cake?" Jacob exclaimed.

Ruth grabbed his hand and pulled him toward the table that now held the cake. "I've got to get a closer look at this," she said.

Alma Lee greeted her with a big hug. Robert stood across the table beaming from ear-to-ear. "So, what do you two think? Alma Lee worked real hard yesterday on this little beauty," he said, obviously proud of his wife's baking skills.

Tears welled up in Ruth's eyes. She kissed Alma Lee lightly on the cheek. "You're really some kind of sister. How can we ever repay the two of you for all you've done?"

Alma Lee gave her a thoughtful look. "For starters, the two of you could make me an aunt. I've always wanted to be somebody's aunt."

Ruth turned to Jacob with a sly smile and arched an eyebrow. "What do you say about that, Dr. Holcomb?"

Jacob flushed slightly, looked at the three of them and gave them a sly grin. "Oh, I do believe the good doctor can come up with a prescription for that," he said. They all laughed.

Sitting in the shade with her shoes off and her feet propped up on a nearby chair, Ruth watched as the many dancers kicked up their heels to the lively music. She turned and faced her folks and Jacob. "I don't think I could dance one more step. I do believe I've danced with every man within ten miles of this place."

Jacob leaned back. "This necktie has got to go. He removed the tie, and wiped his sweaty brow with it. "I'd take off my shoes too, but I'm afraid I couldn't get them back on." Jacob placed the rumpled tie on the table. "I don't believe I'll be putting one of these things on for a long time."

Ruth's father spoke up. "I'll second that. Whoever invented those things, didn't much like men."

Ruth was about to comment about the agony of panty hose, when she spotted Pearl heading in their direction. She could hardly believe her eyes. Pearl walked with purpose, her head held high. She wore a pretty flowered dress and a new pair of sensible, low-heeled shoes. Her hair was pulled back in a ponytail with a colorful ribbon. Clutched in her hands was a vase with the largest bouquet of flowers Ruth had ever seen. When Pearl caught Ruth's gaze, Pearl broke out in a huge grin. She stopped in front of Ruth and handed her the bouquet. "Ruth, I didn't know what I could give ya fer a weddin' present, but just this mornin', I remembered how good I felt when ya brung me that bunch of flowers. I hope ya like 'em. I growed them myself."

Ruth put the flowers in the center of the table. She stood and embraced Pearl in a warm hug and whispered in her ear. "Pearl, those are the prettiest flowers I've ever seen. You picked the perfect present to make this day extra special."

Ruth held Pearl out at arms length. "Would you look at you? You look so pretty in your new outfit. Is that a little bit of makeup I see?"

Pearl blushed and looked down at her feet. "I figured that if I was a comin' to yer weddin', I'd come proper dressed, and a little color wouldn't hurt none."

Jacob interrupted, "Excuse me Ruth. Why don't you introduce Pearl to your folks?"

"What was I thinking?" Ruth gushed, "Mom, Dad, this is a good friend of mine, Pearl. I met her earlier this year when Jacob and I went to check on her husband, Homer. He'd cut his leg real bad. We've become real good friends. Pearl, why don't you sit for awhile? Tell us what you've been doing since I last saw you. I suspect it has been a couple of months since we last talked."

"I can spend a little time with ya, but I promised Homer I would dance with him, and ya know how fidgety he gits," Pearl said.

Jacob's ears perked up when he heard about Homer dancing. "I take it Homer's leg is much better these days, Pearl?"

"Yep, ya fixed his leg right good an' he's back ta cuttin' post an' rails agin. He's even been workin' on fixin' up the house, too. He says that doc's woman done wonders fer me with that bunch of flowers, an' it was 'bout time fer him to do his part."

Ruth's mother, who'd been quietly listening to their conversation, spoke to Pearl. "Are you saying that because my daughter brought you a bouquet of flowers, your life has gotten better?"

"It shore has. We don't hardly git visitors up in our part of the holler and a visit from another woman who brought me flowers was a right big thing ta happen fer me. Homer could see the difference right off. He figured we'd lived in pity of losin' our children long enough, and it was time ta git back ta livin' proper."

Ruth put her hand on Pearl's. "I'm so glad to hear this, Pearl. I never realized that sharing something so small could do such great things."

Pearl's face lit up. "That's only the half of it. Ya knowed 'bout the new, young school teacher we hired fer the holler school, Miz Beth. Well, it turns out that she needed help ta git started with the extra kids we have, so I have been workin' with her fer the last month. It shore is good ta be around younguns, once agin."

"That's really great, Pearl," Ruth said. "I haven't had the pleasure of meeting her. Would you point her out to me?"

Pearl stood, shaded her eyes and surveyed the crowd. "There she is, and just as I thought. Y'ur kin, Win, has her corralled, all ta himself. I've seen him out here jest 'bout every weekend that he can git away from that school he goes ta. I do believe they could be gittin' serious 'bout one another. Who knows, we jest might be back to this here chapel right soon."

Ruth looked over at Jacob. A surprised smile spread across their faces. Ruth held up both hands with her fingers crossed. Jacob rubbed his chin in deep thought. "Hmmm," he said, "I wonder if his mom and dad know about this?"

After the wedding cake had been cut, the newlyweds were ushered through a shower of rice to the waiting carriage.

Ruth and Jacob sat on the padded bench seat and waved vigorously to the wedding guests. Hillard slapped the reins to the rear of the mule. The mule started off at a slow pace, dragging a bunch of tin cans tied behind the carriage. The cans kicked up dust along the dirt road. The mule quickened its pace as several dogs joined the procession, barking and biting at the string of cans trying to tear them loose. They tired of the game quickly and retreated to lie in the shade of the serving tables, waiting for any tasty morsel that might come their way.

Jacob, with his arm around his new bride, held her tight as they traveled the short distance to their honeymoon cabin. Time stood still as they kissed and spoke softly, sharing the joy of the day and their love for one another. The magic of the moment was broken when the carriage lurched to a stop and Hillard hollered out, "Whoa." Jacob jumped from the wagon and helped his new bride down. He then looked up at his old friend and extended his hand. "Hillard, I don't know how I'll ever repay you for all you have done for us."

Hillard gave him a boyish grin. "Ya know what I always say. 'We is holler folks an' we take care of our own.' By the way, the cabin is stocked with food. I'll see that yer presents git over ta my place."

The newlyweds stepped back from the carriage as Hillard slapped the reins to the mule. As he drove away, he hollered over his shoulder, "I'll be back in a week ta pick ya up. Take care, ya hear."

They could hear him laughing over the sound of the cans as he drove away, waving his hand high in the air.

Ruth looked around at the familiar sight of the cabin, as they walked hand-in-hand up the path. Her thoughts flashed back to the first time she'd laid eyes on this beautiful setting. She never dreamed the cabin before her would turn out to be her honeymoon cottage.

At the cabin door, Jacob, in one swift and easy motion, scooped Ruth up into his arms. She reached out and released the latch. As the door swung open, Ruth looked him squarely in the eyes. With an impish grin, she asked, "Well, Dr. Holcomb, shall we honor your sister's request?"

Their kiss was long and passionate, as the door swung shut and closed with a click of the latch.

Chapter 26

One year later

"Dad, did you get a chance to talk to the Department of Tourism yesterday?"

"Yes, I did, Win. They wanted to know if we received the brochures they sent out last week."

"We sure did, and you and Mom are really going to like them. The photographer who took the pictures really did a great job. The Village Lodge is on the front cover. He included pictures of the little general store, the school-house and a real pretty picture of the chapel. An aerial view of the holler is on the back. We were real lucky when he took that shot from the air. The trees were at the peak of their fall color and it's spectacular! I believe we're going to get a tremendous number of inquiries about the Village project. The state has placed the brochures in many strategic locations, promoted it on television and included it in the West Virginia tourism magazine."

"That's great Win! I'll grab a copy from the lodge while were at the holler."

Just as Robert put the finishing touches to Win's necktie, Alma Lee hollered up the stairway. "Win, Robert, have the two of you forgotten what's going on today? I don't think Beth will be very happy if you are late for your own wedding, Win. Stop fretting about the holler project and get down here. Charlie and I have everything loaded in the car, but we need some help with the wedding cake."

Robert stepped back to admire his handsome son. He couldn't believe how quickly this day had arrived. "I look at you today as a full-grown man, Win, but it seems like only yesterday when I first held you in my arms. I'm so proud of you, Win. Now, let's get you to the holler and married to my lovely new daughter-in-law, Beth."

Chapter 27

"Ruth, have you checked on Amanda lately?" Jacob asked.

"She's doing just fine in that little crib you made her, Jacob. I do believe the fresh air of the holler and the peacefulness here, agrees with her. She's sleeping just like a three-month old baby should. Stop worrying about Amanda, and put your necktie on. The wedding starts within the hour. You want to look your best, don't you?"

Jacob grimaced as he finished the knot of his tie and mumbled to himself. "I promised myself I wouldn't be wearing one of these darn things so soon. Now! Look at me."

"What did you say?" Ruth asked, as she walked from the bedroom holding Amanda in her arms.

"Nothing. I was just thinking out loud about what a great day this is going to be. The project's finally getting started, Win is marrying Beth, and we got to come out to the holler and see it all happen. What more could anyone possibly ask for?"

"Well, your sister did mention that Amanda shouldn't have to grow up an only child," she said, with a devilish grin and an arched eyebrow.

Jacob stopped dead in his tracks on the cabin steps and gulped. "Maybe we should see if Win and Beth could satisfy her by making her a grandmother."

Ruth took hold of his hand as they walked down the path to the waiting truck. She hummed a low tune as she held Amanda tightly against her. She looked up at him with a teasing grin. "I believe we can discuss this a little later on tonight."

Ruth, Jacob and baby Amanda arrived just as the last guests entered the chapel. "See," Ruth said, "We were almost late with you fretting over that darn necktie."

Her words had no sooner past her lips than Beth, Pearl and Beth's father stepped around the corner of the chapel. Pearl was the first to spot them. She flashed them a bright toothy smile. "Ya'all best git inside. We's jest 'bout ta go in."

Ruth stopped short. "Would you look here, Jacob? We get to see the bride, Beth, her father and Pearl, the maid-of-honor, before the rest of them." Ruth rushed to Beth, gave her a hug and kissed her on the cheek. "You look beautiful, Beth."

Beth smiled brightly. "Thank you, Ruth, but I sure am nervous."

Pearl took Beth's hand. "Ya will be jest fine Beth. Now take a deep breath jest like I've been tellin' ya." Pearl smiled.

Ruth held Pearl at arm's-length. "Why Pearl, look at you. You've got yourself a lovely smile."

Pearl smiled again. "I done got me some of them store-bought teeth. Homer says they look right smart." They all laughed.

Jacob interrupted. "Excuse me, but I do believe there are a bunch of folks and one nervous Win waiting to see you walk down that aisle, Beth." He shook Beth's father's hand and gave Beth and Pearl a quick hug. "Come on Ruth, let's get inside."

Robert and Alma Lee scooted over to make room for Ruth, Jacob and the baby, as they approached the front pew of the church.

"I thought you two would never get here." Alma Lee said.

Ruth rolled her eyes. "If someone hadn't kept fussing with his tie, we'd have been here sooner."

"Ruth," said Alma Lee, "Let me hold Amanda for awhile."

Robert reached out to hold the baby's hand. Amanda quickly latched onto his finger and pulled it toward her open mouth.

"Remember when Win and Charlie used to do that, Robert?" Alma Lee asked. "Now look at our two boys. Charlie, standing next to Win as his best man, and Win waiting nervously for his bride to walk down the aisle. It seems like only yesterday when the two of them were little babies, just like Amanda." She squeezed his hand tightly. "Robert, I'm going to cry. I just know I am."

The organ sprang to life. All eyes turned toward the chapel doorway.

Chapter 28

The back porch door opened with a rush of cool air. Jacob had an armload of firewood. He stepped into the kitchen.

"That coffee and bacon shore smells great, Sis."

Alma Lee looked up from the cook stove and smiled. "It feels just like old times with just the two of us here. I'm glad you suggested we come to the holler last night."

"Me too," he said. "I haven't been back since the wedding. The clinic had been real busy lately. I have really missed my weekly visits."

"Who's been keeping up with the garden?" she asked.

"I told Win and Beth they could have what was left, seeing as how it was too late in the year for a garden of their own. I'm sure that Pearl and the rest of the holler folks will see to it they don't starve. That's just the way it works in the holler, remember?"

Alma Lee laughed. "Yep, I remember well how they pitched in to help us back then. Talking about helping," she said, "where did that slab of bacon and the eggs come from?"

Jacob added several pieces of wood to the fireplace and held his hands to the flames to warm them. "I called Win before we left Cove Mountain. He said he would have Beth drop some off. She sure is a great gal."

"That she is," Alma Lee said. "Win calls me from the lodge when he's not busy overseeing the operation of the village. Once he gets to talking about Beth and how great married life is, I can hardly get a word in edgewise." She chuckled. "Now, let's eat this food before it gets cold. Win's got a lot to show us today and I can't wait to see how things are coming along."

"From what he's told me," Jacob said, "things have really changed since we last visited."

A flutter of brightly colored leaves blew in front of the truck and scattered about, as a cool wind chased them down the hollow.

Jacob craned his neck and looked up at the nearly bare treetops. "It looks like fall is just about over," he said. "Do you remember the day when Hillard brought us back to the holler after your surgery?"

"I've recalled that day many times over the years," she said. She swallowed hard to hold back her tears. "We came back to what we knew best and a holler that was full of life. Now, thanks to the project and a lot of hard work, holler life has been given a second chance."

Jacob nodded his head and patted her on the leg.

The truck lurched to a stop. Jacob pointed to a spot just past a grove of trees. "Alma Lee, look over there. That building wasn't there three months ago."

"I see it," she said. "Isn't that Hillard standing out front with those other fellows?"

Hillard looked in their direction when he heard the truck doors close. He waved them over. He gave them one of his trademark smiles as he hugged Alma Lee and lifted her with ease, high off the ground. He set her down and wrapped his massive arms around their shoulders. "What is the two of ya doin' out here so early in the mornin'?"

"Win gave us a call to come see the new construction and look in on some of the classes," Jacob answered.

"I haven't been back since Win and Beth's wedding," Alma Lee said.

"That shore was one fine weddin' an' a right smart gatherin'. My Emily cried the entire ceremony," Hillard said.

Alma Lee looked him in the eye, smiled and teasingly said, "Just Emily, Hillard?"

Hillard blushed and averted his eyes. "Well, I mighta shed a tear or two."

Alma Lee wrapped her arms around the impressive girth of his waist and hugged him tight. "That's my Hillard." She laughed.

Jacob put his hand on Hillard's shoulder. "You going to show us this building, or talk us to death."

"Yep," Hillard said. "We's got her 'bout ready ta go."

"I see you've got the roof shingled with oak shakes," said Alma Lee. "Is she water tight?"

Hillard smiled. "She's as tight as a tick on a coon dog."

"Did you rive out the shakes, Hillard?" asked Jacob.

"Nope, Homer rived out every last shake in the village. That old boy sure is handy with a froe and mallet. He's so good at it, Win hired him ta teach a class on it, along with splitin' rails an' such. Come on in an' take a look." Hillard ducked his head as he entered the building. "Mind y'ur footin'", he said, "we's still workin' on that there step."

Jacob stepped into the spacious room. He walked to the closest corner and ran his hand over the logs. "Hillard, I haven't seen such fine cuts on these corner joints since I watched Paw do it."

Hillard patted the nearest log and leaned against the wall and crossed his arms. "They best be good," he said with a smile, "y'ur paw done taught me proper."

"I didn't know that," Alma Lee said. "Paw never mentioned it to me."

"Well, ya was just a young'un when I helped him build the addition to y'ur cabin. "Y'ur paw helped me build my place just before I got hitched ta my Emily, too."

"Paw sure would be proud of all the work you've done at the village," said Jacob. "Win told me you will be here full-time, building and teaching your trade."

"Yep," Hillard said, as he hooked his thumbs in the straps of his faded overalls. "Emily said it was 'bout time I give up that sawmill of mine an' git busy with showin' younguns all I knowed 'bout buildin'." He removed his old felt hat, scratched his head and grinned. "She also said an old man in his sixties don't need ta be gittin' up on any more roofs." He chuckled and jammed his hands deep into the pockets of his overalls.

One of Hillard's young helpers stuck his head through an open window. "Hillard, what ya want us ta do next?"

"I'll be there in a minute," he said.

"We need to get going," said Alma Lee. "Do you know where Win is, Hillard?"

"Last time I seen him, he was over at the woodworkin' shop. I believe they've got a class goin' on 'bout now. Come on, I'll walk out with ya."

Hillard slapped Jacob on the back. "I'll catch up with ya latter, Jacob," he said as he lumbered off toward his waiting crew.

The ring of the blacksmith's hammer against the steel anvil echoed throughout the village. The pungent odor of the forge's burning coal hung heavy in the cool morning air. The high-pitched whine of a chainsaw sliced through the air from high on the mountain side.

"Listen to that, Jacob," Alma Lee said.

"Listen to what?" he asked.

"Everything," she said. "All those familiar sounds we grew up with. It's the sound of progress, hard work and just plain good living." She placed her hand on his arm. "Can you feel the energy that is all around us? It's the holler coming back to life."

Jacob took hold of her hand. "I agree. It's an awesome feeling, Sis, isn't it? Come on. Let's go find that son of yours."

At every turn in the path, they came upon groups of people gathered noisily around the craft buildings. Their enthusiasm for being there was obvious from their laughter and animated conversations.

Jacob and Alma Lee offered smiles and morning greetings as they passed them by.

Jacob turned to Alma Lee. "It sure feels good to see the village come to life."

"I know what you mean," Alma Lee said. "I've prayed long and hard for this day to come."

The path turned sharply around a small grove of trees. Standing fifty feet away was Win. Win spotted them first. "Hey, you two, come on over here. I've got someone I want you to meet." Win walked toward them, a stranger at his side. The young man appeared to be in his late twenties. He sported a full beard and a long ponytail. He was slight of stature. His checkered flannel shirt was threadbare at the elbows and his well-worn jeans had seen better days.

"Mom, Uncle Jacob, I want you to meet one of our newest instructors, Tom. He teaches all forms of woodworking."

Tom stuck out his calloused hand. Jacob shook it with a firm grip. "It's a pleasure to meet you, Tom. I'm Jacob Holcomb and this is my sister Alma Lee."

The introduction hit Tom like a lightning bolt. His large hazel eyes gleamed with excitement and a warm, friendly smile spread across his face. "It's you!" he said. "You're the brother and sister who grew up in the holler and the ones who got all of this started. I can't tell you how proud I am to finally meet you. Win never tires of telling everyone your story." Tom took a step back and ran his hands through his hair. "You guys are . . . legends."

Jacob and Alma Lee beamed brightly at the lavish praise. Alma Lee gained her composure and chuckled. "I don't know about the legend thing, Tom, but I can say for sure, we are pleased you have chosen to share in our dream of preserving the holler way of life." She reached out and gave him a big hug. "Welcome to the holler, Tom."

Tom looked over her shoulder as a noisy group of young men walked toward them. "It looks like my class of future woodworkers has arrived."

"Don't let us hold up progress, Tom," Alma Lee said. "We'll have plenty of time to talk later."

"I'd like to see some of your finished woodworking projects, Tom," said Jacob. Tom stopped in the doorway of the log workshop. "I have some at the main lodge. Win can point them out to you." He waved and disappeared inside.

Win looked at the two of them. "Well, what do you think?"

"I'll say one thing," said Jacob, "he has a great personality and from the feel and strength of his handshake, he's a hard worker."

Win turned to Alma Lee. "What do you think, Mom?"

"I agree with your uncle, Win. I'm confident you picked the right person for the job."

Win smiled. "Oh yeah," Win said, "just you wait until you see his woodcarvings. I've got a lot more to share about Tom, so let's head to the lodge. I'll tell you on the way."

"I'm sure that whatever it is, Win, it will all be good," said Jacob.

"I believe the two of you will be well pleased," Win said.

"Tom was one of the first to apply for permanent living in the holler. He's married and has two children, a boy and a girl. When they first arrived, I drove them around the holler. We looked at many of the vacant cabins, but none seemed to impress them. When we passed by Granny Harris's place, he asked to stop and look it over. I must say, I was surprised at how deteriorated it had become from being vacant for so long. Despite its condition, Tom and his wife fell in love with it. Their enthusiasm for what could be done to fix it up was contagious. I couldn't think of anyone more deserving to live there than a man with Tom's talents."

"I believe you made a wise decision, Win," said Jacob. I know Granny would be pleased that you have a young family living there. You know how she loved children."

Win smiled. "You should stop and see what he's done to the place. He has even carved a plaque and placed it next to the front door. It reads: 'Granny's Place,' along with the dates of her birth and passing."

"I'd like to see that," Alma Lee said. "Let's stop on the way back to the cabin, Jacob."

"Sounds good to me."

When the lodge came into view, Jacob stopped and pointed. "Alma Lee, would you look at how they've fixed up the back porch of the lodge?"

"I decided that visitors should have a comfortable spot to relax and just sit and look out over the village," said Win. "Hillard made all of the log benches for us."

"It looks like he did a fine job." said Jacob.

Win opened the back door and stepped into the lodge. "Come on in and look around," he said. I'll put on a fresh pot of coffee. You can see that we have a good selection of the items our craftsmen have made. There's some pottery, baskets, quilts and much more. We've sold a lot of stuff since we opened for business."

Win turned toward his office and stopped in mid-stride. "By the way, don't forget to check out the front entrance. Some of Tom's impressive carvings are out there."

Alma Lee grabbed Jacob's hand. "Come on. Let's check out the carvings first. I want to see what kind of work Tom does."

"Do I have a choice?" he asked, as she opened the door and stepped out onto the large, covered porch.

To the left of the doorway stood a full-sized eagle, carved from a single block of wood. Jacob knelt in front of the carving and ran his fingers over the intricate cuts.

"Alma Lee, would you look at this?" Silence followed. Then he felt her hand on his shoulder.

"Jacob, come on over by the railing for a minute."

He stood up and followed her to the railing.

Alma Lee turned, leaned against the railing and nodded in the direction of the doorway. "Look there," she said.

Jacob followed her gaze. And there it was. A hand-carved, wooden plaque above the doorway. He looked at the plaque and then at his sister. Her eyes were moist and her lips moved silently as she read each word carved there.

Welcome to Winder Hollow Folk Art Village.
"A place back up in the mountains apiece, just this side of Heaven."

- Winfred Holcomb

Jacob put his arm around her shoulder and pulled her close. Alma Lee leaned her head against him. "Do you think Maw and Paw would be proud of us?" she asked, as she brushed away the solitary tear that had slide down her cheek.

Jacob squeezed her gently. "I do believe they would be right proud, Alma Lee, right proud!"

Richard F. McClure is the author of *The Ragamuffins*. He left the corporate world behind and moved his young family to a self-sufficient lifestyle on a West Virginia mountain top. The memories of those days are woven into the fabric of his writing. He resides with his wife in Florida.

There are no second chances for life versus death in the remote hollows of the Appalachian Mountains. Alma Lee Holcomb, a young woman of sixteen and her younger brother, Jacob, find this out when a tragic accident takes the lives of their parents, Winfred and Grace. Their lives are turned upside down, far beyond anything imaginable. Setting their grief aside, they immerse themselves into the task of surviving, within the isolation of Winder Hollow, but their triumph over adversity is short-lived. When Alma Lee is confronted with a life-threatening illness, they are forced out of the hollow, into a modern world that is completely foreign to them.

Courage, and an undying bond between brother and sister serve them well in the modern world. They make their way in this uncharted territory, while never abandoning their humble beginnings and the mountains they love.

Jacob and Alma Lee come full circle when they return to Winder Hollow. The culmination of their dedication to a dream ends in a wave of emotions, as a memory from the past is revealed.

LaVergne, TN USA
07 April 2010
178385LV00005B/1/P

9 781426 927065